Oliver's Bride

A true Story

Mrs. Oliphant

Oliver's Bride: A true Story

Copyright © 2021 Bibliotech Press
All rights reserved

The present edition is a reproduction of previous publication of this classic work. Minor typographical errors may have been corrected without note; however, for an authentic reading experience the spelling, punctuation, and capitalization have been retained from the original text.

ISBN: 978-1-63637-436-9

CONTENTS

CHAPTER

CHAPTER I

'I have not been always what I ought to have been,' he said, 'you must understand that, Grace. I can't let you take me without telling you, though it's against myself. I have not been the man that your husband ought to be, that is the truth.'

She smiled upon him with all the tenderness of which her eyes were capable, which was saying much, and pressed the hands which held hers. They had just, after many difficulties and embarrassments and delay, said to each other all that people say when, from being strangers, they become one and conclude to part no more. They were standing together in all the joyful agitation and excitement which accompany this explanation—their hearts beating high, their faces illuminated by the radiance of the delight which is always a surprise to the true lover, even when to others it has been most certain and evident. Their friends had known for weeks that this was what it was coming to; but he was pale with the ineffable discovery that she loved

1

him, and she all-enveloped in the very bloom of a blush for pure wonder of this extraordinary certainty that he loved her. She looked at him and smiled, their clasped hands changing their action for the moment, she pressing his in token of utmost confidence as his hitherto had pressed hers.

'I do not mean only that I do not deserve you, which is what any man would say,' he resumed, after the unspoken yet unmistakable answer she had made him. 'The best man on earth might say so, and speak the truth. No man is good enough for such as you; but I mean more than that.'

'You mean flattery,' she said, 'which I would not listen to for a moment if it were not sweeter to listen to than anything else in the world. You don't suppose I believe that; but so long as you do—'

Her hands unloosed and melted into his again, and he resumed the pressure which became almost painful, so close it was and earnest.

'Dear,' he said, with his voice trembling, 'you must not think I mean that only. That would be so were I a better man. I mean that I am not worthy to touch your dear hand or the hem of your garment. Oh, listen: I have not been a good man, Grace.'

She released one of her hands and put it up softly and touched his lips.

'All that has been is done with,' she said, 'for both of us—everything has become new—'

'Ah,' he said, 'if you are content with that, it is so; it shall ever be

2

so. Yet I would not accept that peace of God without telling you—without letting you know—'

'Nothing,' she said, 'or I might have to confess, too.'

'You,' he cried, seizing her in his arms with a kind of rage. 'Oh, never name yourself in such a comparison. You don't know, you can't imagine—'

Once more she stopped his mouth.

'No more, no more; we are both content in what is, and happy in what is to come.'

'Happy is too mild a word. It is not big enough, nor strong enough for me.'

She smiled with the woman's soft superiority to the man's rapture that makes her glad. Superiority yet inferiority, admiring, yet half disdaining, the tide that carries him away—all for her, as if she was worth that! proud of him for the warmth of passion of which she is not capable, at which she shakes her head, not even he able to transport her to such a height of emotion as that to which she, only she, no other! can transport him. She began to be his critic and counsellor on the moment, as soon as it had been acknowledged that she was his love, and was to be his wife.

It had been a long wooing, much interrupted, supposed to be hopeless. They had loved each other as boy and girl seven or eight years before. It is to be hoped that no one will be wounded by the fact that Grace Goodheart was twenty-five; not an innocent angel of eighteen, but a woman who had her own opinions of the world. He was five years older. When she was seventeen and he twenty-two there had been passages between them which he had perhaps forgotten: but she had never forgot. At that period they were both poor. She an orphan girl in the house of her uncle, who was very kind to her, but announced everywhere that he did not intend to leave her his fortune; he a young man without any very definite intentions in life, or energy to make a way for himself. They had parted then without anything said, for Oliver was a gentleman, and would not spoil the future of the girl whom he could not ask to marry him. He had gone away into the world, and he had forgotten Grace. But there is nothing that a girl's mind is more apt to fix upon than the vague conclusion, which is no end, of such an episode. There is in it something more delicate than an engagement which holds the imagination as fast as any betrothal. He has not spoken, she thinks, for honour's sake. He has gone away, like a true knight, to gain fame or fortune, and so win her: and she is consciously waiting for him for long years, perhaps, till he comes back, following him with her heart, with her eyes as far as she can, ever open to all that is heard of him, collecting diligently every scrap of information. Grace had not been without her little successes in that time; others had seen that she was sweet as well as Oliver Wentworth; but she was so light-hearted and cheerful that no one could say it was for Oliver's sake, or for any reason but because she did not choose, that she would have no one in her own sphere. And then came that strange reversal of everything when the old uncle died without any will, and Grace, who it was always supposed must go out governessing at his death, was found to be his heiress. She was his next of kin; there was nobody even to divide it with, to fight for a share; and

4

instead of being a little dependent orphan, she was an heiress and a very good match. How it was that Oliver Wentworth came back after this, was a question that many people asked; but however it was, it was not with any mercenary thought on his part. Whether his sister was equally disinterested, who would take no denial, but insisted on his visit, need not, perhaps, be inquired. He had come rather against his will, knowing no reason why Trix should be so urgent; and then he had met Grace Goodheart, whom he had not seen for so many years, again. To her it was a little disappointing that he came back very much as he had gone away, without having achieved either honour or fortune. But success is not dealt out in the same measure to every man; and if he had failed, how much more reason for consoling him? He had only failed in degree. He had not won either honour or fortune; but he was able to earn his daily bread, and perhaps hers. And when he saw her again, his heart had gone back with a bound to his first love, although in the meantime that love had been forgotten. She was aware, more or less, of all this. She was even aware, more or less, of what he had wanted to tell her. She had followed him too closely with her heart not to know that he had not always kept himself unspotted from the world. This had cost her many a secret tear in the years which were past, but had not altered her mind towards him. There are women who can cease to love when they discover that a man is unworthy; indeed, it is one of the commonplaces both of fact and fiction, that love cannot exist without respect. It would be very well for the good people, and very ill for those who are not good, if this were always so. There are many, many, of women, perhaps the majority, who are not so high-minded, and who love those they love—God help them—whether they

5

are worthy of love or not. Grace was one of those women. She heard, somehow—who can tell how, being intent to hear anything she could pick up about him—that he had not kept the perfect way. She heard that he had gone wrong, and perhaps heard no more for a year or two, and in her secret retirement wept and prayed, but made no outward sign; and then had heard some comforting news, and then again had been plunged into the anguish of those who know that their beloved are in misery and trouble, yet cannot lift a finger to help them. When he appeared again within her ken, she knew it was a man soiled with much contact of the world that met her, and not the pure-hearted boy of old. But he was still Oliver Wentworth, and that was everything. And when in honour and honesty he would have told her how unworthy he was, her heart leapt up towards him in that glory and delight of approbation which is perhaps the highest ecstacy of a woman. His confession, which she would not allow him to make, was virtue and excellence to her. She was more proud of him because he wanted to tell her that he was a sinner, and acknowledge his unworthiness, than if he had been the most unsullied and excellent of men.

Wentworth's sister had always been Grace's friend. She was older than either of them, married, and full in the current of her own life. When Oliver came back to her after all was settled, and made what he believed was a revelation to her of his love and happiness, Mrs. Ford laughed in his face, even while she shared his raptures.

'Do you think I don't know all that?' she said. 'There never was anything so stupid as a man in love. Why, I have known it for the last eight years, and always looked forward to this day.'

Which, perhaps, was not quite true, and yet was true in a way. For Trix had all along loved Grace for loving her brother, and had seen that, with such a wife, Oliver would be all that could be desired; yet had thought it best policy, on the whole, till Grace came into her fortune, to keep them out of each other's way.

'Trix,' he said very gravely, pulling his moustache, 'for eight years she has always been the first woman in the world for me.'

At which his sister, which was very unbecoming, continued to laugh. 'The first, perhaps, dear Noll,' she said, 'but we can't deny, can we, that there have been a few others—secondary? But you may be sure, so far as I am concerned, Grace shall never know a word of that.'

Oliver did not take the matter so lightly. From his rapture of content he dropped into great gravity and walked about the room pulling at his moustache, which was a custom he had when he was thinking. 'On the contrary,' he said, 'I should have liked her to know before she took the last step that—that I haven't been a good fellow, Trix.'

'Oliver, I shouldn't like to hear any one else say so. Tom says' (this was her husband) 'that you've always been a good fellow in spite of—'

'In spite of what?'

'Well, in spite of—little indiscretions,' said Trix, looking her brother in the face, though she coloured as she did so in spite of herself.

'That means—' he said, and walked up and down and pulled his

7

moustache more and more. It was a long time before he added, 'There is nothing that makes a man feel so ashamed of himself, Trix, as to feel that a woman like Grace—if there is anyone like her—'

'Oh, nobody, of course!' said his sister.

He gave her a look, half angry, half tender. 'You are a good woman, too; and to think that two girls like you should take a fellow at your own estimate, and pretend to think that he is a good fellow enough after all: as if that were all that her—her husband ought to be.'

'Well, Noll,' said Mrs. Ford, 'it is better not to go into details. Very likely we should not understand them if you did, though I am no girl, nor is she a baby either, for the matter of that; but whatever you have been or done, the fact is that you are just Oliver Wentworth, when all is said: and as Oliver Wentworth is the man Grace has been fond of almost since she was a child, and who has been my brother since ever he was born—'

'Strange!' he cried, with a curious outburst, half laugh, half groan, 'to think she should have kept thinking of me all this time, while I—'

'Have been in love with her, and considered her all the time the first woman in the world. You told me so just now.'

'Yes,' he said, 'that's not a lie, though you may think it so. I did feel that when I thought of—' and here he paused and gave his sister a guilty look.

'When you thought of her at all; you needn't be ashamed, Noll.

8

That's the man's way of putting it. We women all know that; but now that she is before your eyes and you cannot help thinking of her—now it has come all right.'

Trix too gave a laugh which was half crying; and then she dried her eyes and came solemnly up to him with a very serious face, and caught him by the arm and looked into his eyes.

'Oliver, now that all that's over, and you're an older man and understand that life can't go on so; and now that you are going to marry Grace, the woman you have always loved—Oliver, for the love of God, no more of it now.'

He gazed at her for a moment with a flash of something like fury in his eyes, and then flung her arm far from him with fierce indignation. 'Do you think I am a brute beast without understanding?' he cried.

9

CHAPTER II

For a week or more after their betrothal these two lovers were very happy. To be sure there was a great deal of remark and some remonstrance addressed to Grace about the antecedents of the man she was going to marry. Various people spoke to her, and some even wrote, which is a strong step, asking her if she was aware that Oliver Wentworth had been supposed to be 'wild' or 'gay,' or something else of the same meaning. It is generally supposed that a village or a small town is the place for gossip, but I think Society is made up of a succession of villages, and that there is no place, not even London itself—that wilderness, that great Babylon—in which people are not talked about by their Christian names, and everything that can be discussed, with perhaps a little more, is not known about them. Ironborough was a very large town, but the Wentworths and the Goodhearts had both been settled there for a generation or two, and they were known to everybody. And not only was it known universally and much talked of that Oliver Wentworth had been

10

'wild,' and that he was poor, and consequently that he must be marrying solely for money; but it also raised a great ferment in the place that he should intend, instead of settling down ('and thankful for that') in Grace's charming house, which her old uncle, a man very learned in the art of making himself comfortable, had made so perfect—to carry off his wife to London with him, and live there for the advantage of his work, forsooth! as if his work could be of any such consequence in the ménage, or as if he would ever earn enough to pay the house rent. Oliver was like so many other young men, a barrister with very little to do. He had managed to keep himself going by a few briefs and a little literature, as soon as he had fully convinced himself, by the process of spending everything else that he could lay his hands upon, that a man must live upon what he can make. He was not of so fine a fibre as some heroes, who feel themselves humiliated by their future wife's fortune, and whom the possible suspicion of interested motives pursues everywhere; but at the same time he was not disposed to be his wife's dependent, and he knew the world well enough to be aware that with the backing of her wealth he would probably make a great deal more of his profession than it had hitherto been possible for him to do. As for Grace herself, she talked of his profession, and of his work, and of the necessity for living where it would be most convenient to him, as if her entire fortune depended upon that, and Oliver's work was to be the support of the new household. A girl without a penny, whose marriage was to promote her to the delightful charge of a house of her own, and whose every new bonnet was to come from the earnings of her husband, could not have been more completely absorbed in

11

consideration of all that was necessary for his perfect convenience in his work. She bewildered even Mrs. Ford by the way she took up this idea.

'I honour you for what you say, and I love you for it, Grace; but still you know Oliver's profession is not what you would call very—lucrative, is it? and he could do his writing anywhere, you know!'

'Indeed, I don't know anything of the kind,' said Grace, indignantly. 'He has to be constantly in the House when it is sitting. He has to know everything that is going on. Would you think your husband was well treated if he was made to manage his work, say from the seaside or a country house, for your sake and the children's, instead of being on the spot? You know you would not, Trix.'

'Oh, well, perhaps that may be so; but then my husband—' faltered Trix, with a troubled look. She would have said: 'My husband is the breadwinner, and everything depends on him,' but she was daunted by the look in Grace's eyes, and actually did not dare to suggest that Oliver would be in a very different position. Mr. Wilbraham, the solicitor who managed Miss Goodheart's affairs, interfered in the same way, with similar results. She was in a position of almost unexampled freedom for so young a woman. She had neither guardians nor trustees. There was nobody in the world who had a right to dictate to her or even authoritatively to suggest what she ought to do—for the reason that all she had had come to her as it were inadvertently, accidentally, because her uncle, who always said he intended to leave her nothing, had died without a will. Mr. Wilbraham was

12

the only man in the world who had any right to say a word, and he had no real right, only the right of an old friend who had known her all her life, and knew everything about her. He said, when the settlement was being discussed (in which respect Mr. Wentworth's behaviour was perfect—for all that he wished was to secure his wife in the undisturbed enjoyment of what was her own), that he hoped Miss Goodheart meant to remain, when she was married, among her own friends.

'I don't think you would like London after Ironborough,' he said, with perfect sincerity; 'and to get a house like this in town would cost you a fortune, you know.'

'It is not a question of liking,' said Grace, with all the calm of faith; 'of course, we must live where Mr. Wentworth's work requires him to live. He cannot carry on his profession in the country.'

'The country!' said Mr. Wilbraham, with a sneer which his politeness to an excellent client could only soften. 'Does he call this the country? and Mr. Wentworth's profession, if you will permit me to say so, has, so far as I know—'

'It is the country though, you know,' said Grace, preserving her temper, though with a little difficulty, 'though not exactly what you could call fresh fields and pastures new.'

And when he looked up at her, Mr. Wilbraham made up his mind that it was best to say no more. A willful woman will have her way. Perhaps it was only the lavish and tender generosity of her nature, which would let no one see that she was conscious her position was different from that of the majority of women:

13

but I think it went even a little further than this, and that Grace had got herself to believe that Oliver's work was all in all. She talked to him about it, till he believed in it too, and they planned together the localities in which it would be best to look for a house, in a place which should be quiet so that he might not be disturbed, and yet near everything that he ought to frequent and see; a place where they would, have good air and space to breathe, and yet a place where his chambers, and his newspaper office, and the House should be easily accessible; in short, just such a house as a rising barrister, who was at the same time a man of letters, ought to have. Grace, especially, was very anxious that it should not be too far away. 'As for me, you know, it does not matter a bit—one place is just the same as another to me; but everybody says a man's work loses when he is not always on the spot,' she said. Sometimes Oliver himself was tickled by her earnestness; but she was so very much in earnest that he fell into her tone, and did not even venture to laugh at himself, which was a thing he had been very apt to do.

And those consultations were very sweet. It is doubtful whether anything in life is so sweet as the talks and anticipations of two who have thus made up their minds to be one, while as yet life keeps its old shape, the shape which they feel they have outgrown, and all is anticipation. Everything loses a little when it is realised. No house, to give a small example, is ever so convenient, so delightful, so entirely adapted for happy habitation, as the one which these two reasonable people actually hoped to find To be Let in London. It was to have a hundred advantages which never come together; it was to be exactly at the right distance from the turmoil of town; it was to

14

have rooms arranged just in this and that way; it was to be very capable of decoration, and yet to have a character of its own. Oliver's library was to be the best room in the house, and yet the other sitting-rooms were to be best rooms too. 'I will not endure to have you pushed into a dark room, as poor Mr. Ford is,' said Grace. 'The master of the house, on whom everything depends, should always have the best. To be sure poor Mr. Ford does his work in his office, which is some excuse; but your study, Oliver, will tell for so much. You must let me furnish it out of my own head.'

He laughed a little, and coloured, and said, 'Seeing you will probably furnish it out of your own purse, Grace—'

At which she opened her eyes wide, and looked at him, then laughed too, a little, but gravely, as if it were not a subject for a jest, and said, 'Oh, I see what you mean. You mean me to be the accountant, and all that. Well, I am pretty good at arithmetic, Oliver; and, of course, it might disturb your mind while you are busy, and I shall have nothing else to do.'

This was the way she took it, with a readiness of resource in parrying all allusions to her own wealth which was infinite, though whether she succeeded in this by dint of much thought, or whether it was entirely spontaneous, the suggestion of the moment, no one could quite make out. The result upon Oliver, as I have said, was that he began to believe in himself, too. Instead of laughing at his brief business, which had been his custom, he began to take himself and his work very seriously, and to think how he should apportion his time so as not to leave Grace too much alone—as if he had ever found any difficulty in finding time for whatever he wished to do! 'It is a pity,' he said, 'that this season is just the busiest time, both in chambers and in politics; but I must make leisure to take you about a little, Grace. To think of taking you about, and seeing everything again, fresh, through your dear eyes, is almost too delightful. Would the time were here!'

'It will come quite soon enough, Oliver. We have not even begun to look for the house yet, and there is all the furnishing and everything to do. Don't you think you had better run up to town and begin operations? We may not be able, you know, just at once, to light upon the house.'

'Don't you think you had better come with me, Grace?'

'I? Oh! Why should I go with you? Surely,' she said, with a laugh and a blush, 'you will be able to do that by yourself.'

'How could I do it by myself? I am no longer myself. I am only half of myself. Come and I shall go; but I am not going to leave myself behind me, and stultify myself. I shall not even be one-half but only a fifth or sixth of myself: for there is you, who is the best part of me, and then my heart, which is next best, and my thoughts, which, along with my heart and you, really make up myself—all the best part.'

'What an intolerable number of selfs!' she said; though, perhaps, it was not very clever, it pleased her in that state of mind in which we are all so easily pleased. She said no more, however, and drew away from him, while he jumped to his feet at the opening of the door. The old butler came in with a letter on a tray. There was something sinister in the look of the letter. It was

16

in a blue envelope, and was directed in a very common, informal hand—Immediate written on it in large letters.

'Please, sir, Mrs. Ford's man has come to say as they don't know if it is anythink of importance; but 'as brought it seeing as immediate's on it, in case it should be business, sir; and here, sir, is a telegram as has come too.'

The butler gave a demure glance at his mistress, who was still blushing a good deal, as she had done when she pushed away the chair.

'Thank you, Jenkins!' said Oliver.

He took the letter and looked at it before he opened it. He thought he had seen the handwriting before, but could not remember where. He felt a little afraid of it; he could not tell why. He turned it over in his hand and hesitated, and would have liked to put it in his pocket and carry it away with him for perusal afterwards. What could be so Immediate as to require his attention now—a bill, perhaps? He ran over the list of possibilities in that way, and did not remember anything.

'What is it, Oliver?' said Grace. 'Haven't you opened it? Oh, but you must open it when it is marked Immediate. It must be business, of course.'

'I should think it's a hoax,' he said slowly, 'a circular, or something of that sort' and crushed it in his hand. Then as she made a little outcry—'Well, I'll open it to please you. All women, I perceive, believe in letters,' he said, with a smile.

The joke was but a small one at the best—it seemed smaller and smaller as he opened the envelope and read what was written within. Grace had gone away to re-arrange some flowers on the table, to leave him at liberty. She bent over them, taking out some that were beginning to fade, pulling them about a little till the moment should be over. It seemed to run into two or three minutes, and Oliver did not say anything or even move. He would generally say, 'Oh, it is So-and-so!'—some friend who sent his congratulations. That was the chief subject of all their letters at the present time. They were letters which were handed from one to another with little notes of admiration. 'Poor fellow, he is as pleased as possible.' 'What a nice letter, Oliver! I am sure he must be fond of you,' and so forth, and so forth. But he said nothing about this. To be sure, it was business.

She turned round at last, not knowing what to do; wondering, when your bridegroom does not tell you of a thing, what is your duty in the circumstances. To ask, or to hold your tongue? Grace was not jealous, or ready to take offence. And she was very anxious to do her duty. What ought she to do?

He folded up the letter, as he heard her move, and turned towards her, but without raising his eyes. His face was clouded and dark. He put it into his pocket, and they sat down and began to talk, but not as before, though of the same subject.

At last he said, abruptly, 'I think I will go up to town, Grace. You suggested it, you know,' as if he had altogether forgotten all that he had said, which she had chidden him for, and loved him for, all that pleasant nonsense about himself.

She was startled for a moment; then replied quietly, 'Yes, Oliver, I do think it will be the best way—'

18

He continued hesitating—faltering. 'It is not for that only, my darling. This letter—I am afraid I shall have to go: a—a friend of mine has got into trouble. I—can't exactly tell what it is; but wants me to go.'

'Oh, how sorry I am!' said Grace. 'Dear Oliver, it is natural people should turn to you when they are in trouble. Who is he? Do I know him? Has he written to you about—'

'I don't suppose—he—knows anything about it. It is a friend I haven't heard of for a long time. Not one for you to know, but in great trouble. Dying, the letter says.'

'Oh, Oliver, go—go at once. Not for the world would I keep you from a dying man. Don't tell me any more than you wish, dear. But can I do anything—can I send anything? Is he—oh, Oliver, forgive me—is he poor?'

'Forgive you?' he said. He held her close to him with a strain which was almost violent, as if he could not let her go. Then he said, 'No, my darling, you can do nothing. I may have helped to make things worse, and I am at the height of happiness, while this poor creature—this poor—'

'Oh, Oliver, go and comfort him,' she said, 'Don't lose a train; don't come back to any good-bye. Go—go!' Then while he hold her in his arms she said, smiling, 'It need not be a very long parting, I suppose?'

'Any parting is long that takes me from you, Grace.'

'But it is for love's sake. Good-bye. I'll do all I can do, Oliver. I'll pray for you—and him.'

'God bless you, my dear love—not good-bye—till we meet again.'

And then the door closed, and he was gone.

The day had grown dark, surely, all at once. It was a day in early spring, and very cloudy. A mass of dark vapour had blown up over the sweet sky; and what a change it was all in a moment, from that pretty fooling about himself and his other self to this sudden parting! But, then, it was an errand of mercy on which he was going. God be with him! And it could not be for long. Nothing, neither trouble nor suffering, nor death of friends, nor any created thing could separate them long.

CHAPTER III

Trix was not so quickly satisfied as Grace had been. 'Going away!' she cried; 'going to leave Grace! I thought you could not bear to have her out of your sight.'

'I hope I was not such an ass as to say so, but I cannot help myself—it is an old friend—'

'Who is he? Do I know him?' she said, as Grace had said. 'You men are so ridiculous about your friends. Probably somebody that did you nothing but harm, and whom you would be thankful never to hear of again.'

'You speak like an oracle. Trix; but I must go all the same.'

'And why don't you say who he is? Ah, it was a great deal better for you, Oliver, when you had no friends that your sister didn't know of. Tell me who he is—at least, tell me his name.'

'You would not be a bit the wiser. You know nothing whatever about—him. Trix, take great care of her while I am away.'

21

'Oh, as for taking care of her!—' He went out of the room while she was speaking to put his necessaries into his bag. And left alone, she began to think still more doubtfully over the meaning of this sudden move. She ran over every name she could think of, of people whom she knew he had known. She, too, felt the influence of that sudden cloud which blotted out the sky and brought the quick deluge of the spring shower pouring about the ears of the wayfarers. The darkness assisted her womanish imagination, as it had done that of Grace. It was like a sudden misfortune falling when no one thought of it. And Mrs. Ford's mind was greatly exercised. When Oliver came into the room again, ready to start, she got up quickly and went to him with her two hands on the lappels of his coat. 'Oliver,' she cried, breathlessly, 'I hope to goodness it is a him, and not—You couldn't, you wouldn't—it isn't possible.'

'Suspicion seems always possible,' he said, harshly, putting her away from him. Was it the natural indignation of one unjustly blamed? 'If that is all you think of me, what can it matter what I say?'

'Oh,' cried Trix, who was very impulsive, 'I beg your pardon, Noll. It was only that I—it was because I am so anxious, oh, so anxious! that everything should go well. You won't be long—not any longer than you can help?'

'Not a moment,' he said. 'If I can return to-morrow, I will. I hope so with all I my heart. Going at all is no pleasure. Take care of her while I am away.'

It seemed to Trix that he was gone before she had known that he was going. It was very sudden. He had not intended to go at all till after his marriage. He had said so only that morning: and why this change all in an hour? A friend! It must be a very intimate friend, she concluded, or he would not have thrown up all his plans to go and visit him. To be sure, when a man is dying he is not likely to wait the convenience of another who is about to be married. She told her husband when he came in in the evening, and he, a good man, who was not wont to trouble himself about hidden meanings, received the news with great placidity.

'Is it anyone we know?' was his first question. 'I hope it may be the sort of friend who will leave him something—a legacy couldn't come at a better moment.' This was a wonderful sedative to her alarms, and turned her thoughts into quite a different channel. It would be indeed a most suitable moment to have a legacy left him. Every time is suitable for that, but when a man is about to be married, nothing could be more appropriate. Mrs. Ford went across in the evening, after dinner, to see Grace. They lived quite near each other, and the Fords for that evening had no engagement. She found her future sister-in-law sitting over a little, bright fire, reading a novel, with papers beside her on the table, lists from the furniture shops, and some made out in her own handwriting of things that would be required in the new home. Miss Goodheart received Mrs. Ford very cordially. 'It feels so odd to be quite alone again,' she said, with a little laugh, which was slightly nervous, 'and when one didn't expect it. So I was glad to find a new book. Poor Oliver! he will not have pleasant journey. I hope he will find his friend better. Is he a friend of yours, too?'

'He was in such a hurry he had not time to tell me, nor I to ask him,' said Trix, which was not, as the reader knows, quite true.

There was a little pause after this, as if they each would have liked to ask questions of the other; and then, no questions being possible, as neither knew, they plunged into furniture, which is a very enthralling subject. Trix, having experience, was able to give many hints, and to suggest a number of things Grace had left out—kitchen things, for instance. How can anyone know about pots and pans, and how many are necessary, without practical knowledge supplied by recent experience?

They both subdued a little dull pain they had about the region of their hearts by a good long talk on this subject, and parted quite cheerfully when Mr. Ford—who never had any pains in that region except those which are produced by a digestion out of order—came to fetch his wife.

'Oliver will take the opportunity to do several things on his own hook, now that he has managed to tear himself away,' that gentleman said. 'The great difficulty was to tear himself away. And I only hope his friend will leave him something.'

This, though it was so prosaic, gave a real comfort to the two women. It brought his mission quite out from the mystery that hung about it to the range of commonplace affairs.

It was not till Wentworth was fairly gone from the station shut up by himself in a compartment of a first-class carriage, and unapproached by any spectator, that he took out from his pocket and read over again the letter and telegram which had called him away thus hurriedly out of the happiness of his new life.

The letter was on blue paper, not without a suspicion of greasiness, and very badly written in a hand which might have been that of a shopman or a schoolboy. But it was signed by a female name, and this is what it said:—

'Dear Mr. Wentworth,—

'Alice came home in bad health three months ago. She's been very bad ever since, and there is now no hopes of her. It's consumption and heart complaint, and what the doctor calls a complickation. For the last fortnight she's been weaker and weaker every day, and yesterday was took much worse, and hasn't but a day or two to live. She says as she can't die happy without seeing you. She calls for you all the time she's waking, both night and day. Oh, Mr. Wentworth, you always was a kind gentleman, not like some; I know as you would have nothing to say to her if she was well: but being as she's very ill and near her death, I do hope as you'll listen to me. You was the first as she ever took a fancy to, she says. But if you come, oh come at oncet, for there is not a moment to be lost.

'Yours truly,
'Matilda.'

He unfolded the telegram afterwards and read, 'If you want to find her in life, come at once.'

Wentworth remarked with a kind of horrible calm, and even a smile, that the telegraph people had corrected the spelling. This was the summons for which he had left Grace. He had read both

25

more than once. Now that he had obeyed the call, he asked himself was it indeed so necessary—ought he to have done it? There had been perhaps something in the force of the contrast, something in the happiness which was so much more than he deserved, in the purity and nobleness of the woman who had given him her hand, and who was making her spotless atmosphere his, that stung him with that intolerable, remorseful pity, the impulse of which is not to be resisted. Standing by the side of his bride, and on the edge of a life altogether above his deserts, he had felt that he could not resist this appeal to him. To refuse to speak a word of comfort to a dying creature—he to whom God had been so good—how was it possible? Comfort! What comfort could he give? He might bid her repent, as he had repented. But his repentance had been paid, it had been richly recompensed, it was setting open to him the doors of every happiness; whereas to this sharer of his iniquities it was to be followed only by suffering and death.

Wentworth had never been callous or hard-hearted at his worst: and now at his best, compassion and remorse overwhelmed him. That he should receive that information, that appeal, with Grace's hand in his, gave his whole nature a shock. He felt that he must take himself away out of her presence, and remove the recollections, the scenes that rushed back upon his mind, the image thus thrust before his eyes, away from her at least, even if he did not answer the appeal. He was not of the iron fibre of some men. He could not carry these two images side by side.

And then how did he dare resist such an appeal. 'You were the first.' He had said to himself that he was responsible for the ruin

26

of no other human creature. He was not a seducer. He had used no wiles to draw anyone from the paths of virtue. Is that a defence when life and death are in the balance, and a man is arraigned before the tribunal of his own conscience? When he went back into the recesses of his memory and beheld all that was brought before him, as by a flash of lightning, and then remembered the position in which he now stood, he covered his face with his hands. He was ashamed to the bottom of his soul. The way of transgressors is hard. To anyone who had known all the facts, it would have appeared that Oliver Wentworth was the most striking example of undeserved happiness. He had no right to all the good things that had fallen into his lap. He had deserved a very different return for all that he had done; yet when he set out upon that railway journey, with the touch of Grace's hand still warm in his, the shame and misery in his mind were a not unfit representation of those tortures which to most men are more real than the fire and brimstone of the bottomless pit. How was the recollection of what was passed ever to be washed out of his memory? He might repent—he had repented—and never so bitterly as now: but how was he to forget? In the great words of mercy it is proclaimed that God forgets as well as forgives: 'Their sins and iniquities will I remember no more.' But the sinner, how is he to forget, even when he believes that he is forgiven?

Yet, what he was doing was not shameful nor sinful. It was mercy that carried him away from all he loved to give what consolation he could to a dying creature whom he had never loved, who had been but the companion of his amusements for a moment of aberration, a time which he looked back upon with

27

astonishment and disgust. How could he have forgotten himself so far? How could he have fallen into such depths? His mind was so revolted by the recollection, such a horror and loathing filled him at the thought, that it was impossible to suppose that any softer sentiment lay concealed beneath. Had he been a less tender-hearted man, he would probably have thrown the letter into the fire, and perhaps sent a little money as the common salve for all sufferings; but his very happiness and elevation above those wretched recollections took from him the power to dismiss such an appeal in this way. And was it not a certain atonement, at least an offering of painful service such as the heart of man believes in, whatever may be its creed, to do this? The money he could have sent would have cost him nothing— this cost him what was incalculable, a price almost beyond bearing. His agitation calmed a little as he pursued these thoughts. He could not do her any good, poor creature; but if it pleased her, if it eased a little the last steps towards the grave?

He arrived in London late on a wet and cold spring night; in town there was little visible of the shivering growth which makes a sudden chill in spring more miserable than winter; but the streets were wet and gleaming with squalid reflections, and the crowds, even in the busiest thoroughfares, were thinned and subdued. Wentworth took a cab and drove through a part of London with which he was not familiar, through line upon line of poor little streets, each one exactly like its neighbours, lighted with few lamps, with a faint occasional shop window, few and far between, and with only at long intervals a dark figure under an umbrella going up or down. The endless extent of this net-work of streets, all poor, mean, dark, yet decent, the homes of myriads unknown, gave him a sense of weariness that many miles of country would not have produced.

At last the cab stopped before one of the narrow doors, flanked with little iron railings, the usual parlour window over-looking a narrow little area. In the room above a light was burning, and all the rest of the house dark. A square printed advertisement of some trade was in the parlour window, just visible by the lamplight, and a painted board of the same description was attached to the railings. The door was opened by a young woman with a candle in her hand, which nearly blew out with the entry of the blast of night air, and flickered before her face so that it was difficult to make out her features. She gave a little cry, 'Oh, it's Mr. Wentworth!' and bade him come in. To describe the sensation with which Wentworth realised his position, known and expected in this house, going up the narrow stair which was all that separated him from the sickroom, from the dying woman, between whom and himself he was thus acknowledging a connection, is more than I can attempt. There was no secret here—a man in the slipshod dress of a worker at home looked out from the little back room and asked, 'Has he come?' as he passed. On the top of the stairs an older woman, with the dreadful black cap of the elderly decent English matron of the lower classes, came out to meet him, and put out her hand in welcome. 'How do you do, Mr. Wentworth? She's that excited there's no keeping her still: and I'm so glad you've come.'

In the face of all this, his heart sank more and more. He felt himself no longer on a mission of mercy, but going to meet his fate.

CHAPTER IV

The room was small and dingy: opposite to the door an old-fashioned tent-bed hung with curtains of a huge-patterned chintz, immense flowers on a black ground: a candle standing on a small table by the bedside, another faintly blinking from the mantelpiece beyond, the darkness of everything around bringing into fuller relief the whiteness of the bed, the pillows heaped up to support a restless head, a worn and ghastly face, with large, gleaming eyes, which seemed to have an independent, restless life of their own. The face had been pretty when Wentworth had known it first. It was scarcely recognisable now. The cheek bones had become prominent, the lower part of the face worn away almost to nothing, the eyes enlarged in their hollow caves. She looked as she had been said to be—dying—except that the light in her eyes spoke of a secret force which might be fever, or might be because they were the last citadel of life. But though she seemed at the last extremity of existence, a few efforts had been made to ornament and adorn the dying creature, efforts which

30

added unspeakably, horribly, to the ghastly look of her face. The collar of her night-dress had been folded over a pink ribbon, leaving bare an emaciated throat, round which was a little gold chain, suspending a locket: and her hair, still plentiful and pretty, the one human decoration which does not fade, was carefully dressed, though somewhat disordered by the continual motion of her restlessness. It was all horrible to Wentworth, death masquerading in the poor little vanities which were so unspeakably mean and small in comparison with that majesty, and all to please him—God help the forlorn creature! to make her look as when he had praised her prettiness, she from whom every prettiness, every possibility of pleasing, had gone.

She held out her two hands, which were worn to skin and bone, 'Oh, Oliver, my Oliver! oh, I knew he would come. Oh, didn't I say he would come?' she cried. Wentworth could not but take the bony fingers into his own. He saw that it was expected he should kiss her; but that was impossible. He sat down in the chair which had been placed for him by the bedside.

'I am very sorry to see you so ill, my poor girl,' he said.

'Ill's not the word, Mr. Wentworth; she's dying. She hasn't above an hour or two in this world,' said the mother, or the woman who took a mother's place.

He gave her a look of horrified reproach, with the usual human sense that it is cruel to announce this fact too clearly. 'I hope it is not quite so bad as that.'

'Yes, Oliver; oh, dear Oliver, yes, yes,' said the sick woman. 'This is—my last night—on earth.' She spoke with difficulty, pausing

31

and panting between the words, her thin lips distended with a smile, the smile (he could not help remarking) that had always been a little artificial, poor girl! at her best. But even at that awful moment she was endeavouring to charm him still (he felt with horror) by the means which she supposed to have charmed him in the past.

'Tell him, mother, tell him. I haven't got—the strength.' She put out her hands for his hand, which he could not refuse, though her touch made him shiver, and lay looking at him, smiling, with that awful attempt at fascination. He covered his eyes with his disengaged hand, half because of the horror in his soul, half that he might not see her face.

'Mr. Wentworth,' said the elder woman, 'my poor child, sir, she's got one wish—' the bony hands closed upon his with a feeble, yet anxious pressure as this was said.

'Yes; what is it? If it is anything I can do for her, tell me. I will do anything that can procure her a moment's pleasure,' he said.

Fatal words to say! but he meant them fully—out of pity first, and also out of a burning desire, at any cost, to get away. Anything for that! He would have willingly given the half of what he possessed only to get away from this place—to return to the life he had left, to hear this woman's name no more.

Once more the wasted hands pressed his, and she gave a little cry. 'I knowed it—always—mother. I told you.'

'Hush, hush, dear! Don't you wear yourself out. You'll want all your strength. Mr. Wentworth, I didn't expect no less from a

32

gentleman like you. If she hasn't been all she might have been, poor dear! though I don't want to blame you, sir, you're not the one as should say a word—for it was all out of love for you.'

Wentworth had it not in him to be cruel, but he drew his hand almost roughly from between the girl's feverish hands. 'What is the use of entering into such a question?' he said. 'I do not blame her. Let the past alone. What can I do for her now?'

He had risen up, determined to make his escape at all hazards—but the little cry she gave had so much pain in it that his heart was touched. He sat down again, and patted softly the poor hand that lay on the coverlet. 'My poor girl, I don't want to hurt you,' he said.

'You mustn't be harsh to her,' said the mother. 'How would you like to think that poor thing had gone miserable out of this world to complain of you, sir, before the Throne? Not as she'd have the heart to do it, for she thinks there is no one like you, whatever you may say to her. Mr. Wentworth, there's just one thing you can do for her. Make an honest woman of her, sir, before she dies.'

'What!' said Wentworth, springing once more to his feet. He but dimly, vaguely understood what she meant, yet felt for a moment as if he had fallen into an ambush, as if he had been trapped into a den of thieves. He thought he saw a man's head appearing at the door, and heard whisperings and footsteps on the stairs. This it was that produced the momentary fury of his cry; but then he regained control of himself, and looking round saw no one but the dying girl on the bed and an elderly woman

33

standing in front of him, looking at him with deprecating yet earnest eyes.

'It's a great deal,' said the woman, 'and yet it's nothing. It's what will never harm you one way or another, what nobody will know, nor be able to cast in your teeth—that won't cost you anything (except, maybe, a bit of a fee), and yet it's everything to her. It would make all the difference between going out of this world honest and creditable and going in her shame, which it was you that brought her to it.'

'That's a lie!' said Oliver. Was it to be supposed he could think of civility at such a moment? A desperate tremor seized hold upon him. He got up and turned, half blinded with horror and excitement, towards the door. 'I came here,' he said, 'because— because—'

Ah! because—why? What could he say? He had meant to be kind—to make up to her somehow, he could not tell how, for the fact that he was happy and she dying. He stood arrested with those words upon his lips, which he could not say, half turned from her, facing the door, as if he would have broken away.

And then there came a low, despairing cry from the bed—the cry as of a lost creature. 'Oh, Oliver, Oliver! you loved me once. Oh, don't go and leave me! You loved me, and I loved you.'

He would have cried out that it was false, but the breathless voice, broken by panting that sounded like the last struggle, the voice of the woman who was dying, while he was full of life and force, silenced him in spite of himself. The mother had flown to her to raise her head, to give her something from a glass on the table, and he, too, turned again, awe-stricken, thinking the last moment had come.

'And you can stand and see her like this,' said the woman by the bedside, in a low tone. 'You that are well and strong and have the world before you; and let her go out of it at five-and-twenty, a girl as you made an idol of once, a girl as you have helped to bring to this, and won't lift a finger to satisfy her before she dies, to give her what she wants, and what will make her happy for the last hour—before she dies!'

The girl herself was past speaking. She lay back against her mother's breast, her own worn and emaciated shoulders heaving with convulsive struggles for the departing breath. She could not speak, but those eyes, which were so living while she was dying, turned to him with a look of such appeal, such entreaty that he could not bear the sight. They were large with fever and weakness, liquid and clear and dilated, as the eyes of the dying often are, like two stars glowing out in sudden light from the pale night of her face. He cried out, 'What do you want me to do?' with despair in his voice, and a sense that whatever they asked of him he could not now refuse.

'To do her justice,' said the mother. 'Oh, Mr. Wentworth, to make up to her for all she's suffered. To make her an honest woman before she dies.'

The girl's dying lips moved, but no sound was heard: a pathetic smile came upon her lips, her eyes held him with that prayer, too intense for words. Oliver turned away his head not to see them, then turned back again as if in them there was some spell. A

35

passionate impatience pricked his heart, for their inference was not true. They had not been to each other what was said. Love! love was too great a word to be mentioned here at all. It had been levity, folly; it had not been love. She had been too slight for such a word; but she was not too slight for death. For that solemnity nothing is too slight or too poor; and death is as great as love is, and compels respect. She drew his eyes to her so that he could not free himself. He said in an unnatural, stifled voice, 'Whatever you want from me—this is not the—the time. There is nothing to be done to-night—and after to-night'—he could not say the words—he waved his hand towards the bed. She was dying now—now—before their eyes.

'I know what you mean,' said the mother, with dreadful calm. 'She won't last out the night. Very likely she won't, but that's what nobody knows except her Maker. If she don't, you can't do nothing, and nobody here will say a word. But if she do—! Give her your word, Mr. Wentworth, as you'll marry her to-morrow if she lives, and she'll die happy. She'll die happy; whether it comes to anything or whether it don't. Mr. Wentworth, sir, do, for the love of God!'

The girl recovered a little gasping breath. 'I'll die happy. I'll die happy, whether it comes to anything or not.' Even this little rally showed more and more the nearness of the end.

He had shrank at the word 'marry' as if it had been a blow aimed at him, but he could not escape from the tragic persistence of those eyes. And overwhelmed as he was, a little hope rose in him. He said to himself, 'She can never live till to-morrow.' Why should he resist if a promise would make her happy? for she was

36

surely dying, and she never could take him at his word. 'If that is all, I will promise,' he said.

The light in her eyes seemed to give a leap of joy and triumph, then closed under the flickering eyelids, he thought for ever, and he cried out involuntarily, and made a step nearer to the bed. When her eyes were closed, she looked like one who had been dead a day, nothing but a faint, convulsive heave of the shoulders showing that there was life in her still.

The mother busied herself about the half-unconscious creature, putting the cordial to her lips, supporting the pillow against her own breast. 'You will have an easy bargain,' she said, as she went on with these cares; 'but anyhow, we'll bless you for what you say. Matilda, give me the drops the doctor left for her when she felt faint. She's very low, now, poor dear! Mr. Wentworth's behaving like a gentleman, as you always said he would. He has promised to marry her to-morrow morning, if she lives. She'll not live, but she's satisfied, poor dear!'

Matilda had come so softly into the room that she startled him as if she had been a ghost. 'I knew as he would do it when he saw how bad she was; but, Lord, what do it matter to the poor thing now?'

This was his own opinion. In a few minutes more there was a bustle downstairs, which Matilda pronounced to be the doctor coming, and Wentworth went down to wait until he had paid his visit. The little parlour below had one candle burning in it, for the benefit of those who went and came. The young man was left there for a few minutes alone. To describe the condition in

37

which he was is impossible. His heart was beating with a dull noise against his breast. All that had been so bright to him a little while before had become as black as night. He could not think; only contemplate what was before him dumbly, with horror and disgust and fear. He had given a pledge, but it was a pledge that never would call for fulfilment—no, no, it never could be fulfilled—it would be as a nightmare, a dreadful dream, from which he would awake by-and-by and find the sun shining and all well. After a while he heard the doctor's heavy foot come clamping down the wooden staircase. He was angry with the man for having so little delicacy, for making so much noise when his patient was dying. Presently he came in to give his bulletin to the gentleman, whom he perceived at once to be somehow very deeply concerned.

'Last the night? No, I don't think she'll last the night: but you never can tell exactly with such nervous subjects. She might put on a spurt and come round again for a little while.'

'Then,' said Wentworth, with a sense that he was acquiring information clandestinely, 'there is no hope of any permanent recovery?'

The doctor laughed him to scorn. If he had not been a parish doctor, accustomed to very poor patients and their ways, he would not have allowed himself to laugh in such circumstances.

'When she has not above half a lung, and her heart is—but you don't understand these matters, perhaps. She may make a rally for a few hours, but I doubt if she will see out this night.'

After this, Wentworth went home to the closed-up chambers,

38

where nobody expected him, and to which he got admittance with difficulty. He had to walk miles, he thought, through those dreadful streets, all like each other, all gleaming with wet, before he could even find a cab. There was no strength left in him. He went on and on mechanically, and might, he thought, have been wandering all night, but that the sight of a slowly passing cab, which he knew he wanted, brought him back to a dull sense of the necessity of shelter. The cold rooms, so vacant and unprepared, which were just shelter and no more, were scarcely an improvement upon the mechanical march and movement, which deadened his mind and made him less sensible of his terrible position. It had been arranged that if she was still alive in the morning, a messenger was to be sent to him, and that then he was to take the necessary steps to redeem his pledge. But he said to himself that it was impossible—that she could not live till morning. It was a horrible moment for a man to go through—a man whose life had blossomed into such gladness and prosperity. But still, if he could but be sure that nothing worse was to come of it—and what could come of it when the doctor himself was all but sure that she could not see out the night?

CHAPTER V

Oliver spent a disturbed and sleepless night. He went to bed as a form, one of those things that people do mechanically, and because the cold of the shut-up rooms went to his heart. But he was astir very early, before it was daylight. He had not slept but only dozed, miserably repeating in dreams which that film of half sleep made into mere distortions of his waking thoughts, the circumstances of the past evening, the journey, the leave-taking with Grace, the horror at the end. It was a relief to be fully awake and only have reality to contend with, miserable as that was. Dawn came slowly stealing, filtering in marred and broken light through the clouds and the rain which had continued through the night. His whole being was concentrated in expectation of a sound at his door. Every moment which passed without a summons encouraged him. He said to himself, 'It must be all over, all over.' A dozen times the tension of his great excitement seemed to produce a tingling in the silence which simulated the sound of the bell. But it was nothing, and the cold dawn gradually developed into full but colourless day. He was saying to himself for the hundredth time, 'It must be all over,' and feeling for the first time a little ease in his mind as if it might really be so, when suddenly the bell rang. Ah! that was no vibration of excitement in the air; it was the bell, very distinctly, loudly rung, and pealing into the stillness. It rang and echoed into Wentworth's very heart, the brazen tinkle wounding him like a knife, so sudden, so sharp and keen. There was no one to open the door but himself, no one in the place to do anything for him. He did not move for a moment, finding that he needed time to recover from the sting of that blow, when it was repeated more sharply still, not without impatience. It occurred to him, then, that it might be something else than the messenger of fate—the postman, perhaps—some one who had nothing to do with this tragedy. These hopes, if hopes they could be called, were dissipated, however, when he opened the door. Outside stood a young man in shabby clothes with a face which reminded him of poor Alice at her best. 'Mother sent me to tell you that Ally's living and a little better. If you'll come at eleven, she'll have the parson there as visits in our street.'

'If I come at eleven!' Oliver said, with a gasp.

'She said you would understand. I don't know as I do. I think they'd a deal better let you alone. What good can you do her?'

Here seemed a help, an advocate—and Oliver looked at him with an eagerness that was almost supplication. 'That is what I think,' he said; 'what good can I do her? It can only agitate her and hasten the end.'

'Well,' said the young man, 'it's none of my business. Mother and the rest will have it their own way. But as for hastening the end, that's the best thing that could happen, for she do nothing but feel bad lingering there. At eleven o'clock: and to look sharp, for the parson will be waiting, mother says. 'Good-morning!' the youth said, turning quickly and going off down the stairs. He began to whistle after a few steps, then stopped, briefly, with an oh! of recollection, as if remembering that to whistle was indecorous in the present position of affairs.

Oliver went back to his cold and empty rooms with a sense that life was over and his heart dead within him. It seemed to fall down to some impossible depths, down to a grave of silence and darkness. He shut the door mechanically, and went back and sat down where he had been sitting before, and stared with blank eyes in front of him into the vacant air. God had not interposed to deliver him. But why, he asked himself, should God have interposed? God had not been consulted or referred to in all this connection—in anything that had passed—and why, unasked, undesired, should He step in now like a heathen god or a tutelary deity to set all right? Oliver did not feel that he could make any appeal even to Him who was all righteousness and purity to help him out of the consequences of his own folly and sin. Oh, yes, it was true many men had done as much whom no judgment overtook, who lived fair before the world, and had no shame put upon them, and forgot that they had ever stepped aside from the paths of virtue. He had himself almost forgotten—almost—till contact with a purer life and the gift of it to be his companion, and all the happiness to which he had so little right, had brought compunction to his soul. He remembered now how he had told Grace that he had not been a good man: and how she had stopped him as the father in the parable stopped the Prodigal in his confession—she had stopped him, putting her pure hand upon his lips, throwing her whiteness over him like a mantle. But there had been judgment waiting behind. Justice had been standing watching his futile attempts at escape, with a face immovable, holding her scales. He had been weighed and found— — ah, no one but himself knew how entirely wanting! And now here was the price to pay. He had promised and he could not escape.

After a moment he tried to say to himself that these solemn thoughts were inappropriate, that after all it was not much of a matter—to please a dying woman, whom he had been supposed to love once—to give her a little pleasure, poor soul! a little poor mimicry of pleasure on the day of her death; where was there a man so hard-hearted that would not do that? And then he had not any time to think; if he were to fulfil this miserable appointment, he must do what was necessary at once. He rose and got his bank-book out of its drawer and looked over it carefully, calculating how much he had. He had gone over the calculation so often, enough for the wedding trip which Grace and he had arranged to make, and in which, at least, he felt that her money must not be touched. He had enough for that and to pay a few little debts, those little foolish things that accumulate without thinking—enough to wind up everything honourably and start fair. He seemed to be tearing the heart out of his breast when he tore out the cheque which he must presently pay for a special licence—a licence! to marry, Heaven help him! to marry: he who was the bridegroom of Grace Goodheart, his name already publicly linked with hers. The horror of these names and words gave him each a new sting and stab; but what were words in comparison with the thing which he was about to do? He set out presently, pale, with his eyes red like those of a midnight reveller, his face haggard with misery, with want of rest and food and sleep, and got a cab and drove to the place where the licence had to be procured. That done, he turned his face again to the monotonous, endless streets, the dismal, shabby quarter where his business was. Finding he had a little time to spare, he dismissed the cab, and walked and lost himself in the fathomless maze, and arrived late at the house. The young woman, Matilda, was standing at the door looking out for him, the youth who brought the message stood within the area rails, the mother, with the blind a little polled aside in the room above, was looking out too. There was a ray of pleasure and welcome when he appeared.

'I knew as you'd come,' cried Matilda, 'and so did she: but mother was frightened a bit, not knowing you, Ol—Mr. Wentworth like her and me—' Oliver grew sick as he stepped into the narrow passage. The half-sound of his own name, which she had not ventured to pronounce fully, seemed to open another vista before him. He would be Oliver to this woman, too—a member of the family. He went in, scarcely knowing where he went. In the parlour was the clergyman, who met him severely, saying that he had been kept waiting for nearly half-an-hour.

'And my time is precious; not like that of an idler.' He was a severe young man in the High Church uniform, thin and meagre with overwork and earnestness. 'I am glad,' he said, 'that you have made up your mind to do justice to your victim at the last.'

44

'My victim!' said Oliver.

But what was the use of any explanation? He began to recognise that in ordinary parlance she was his victim, and that it might be considered an act of justice; and also that to explain to a severe purist, a man burning with the highest canons and sentiments of morality, how such a thing could be without any victim in the matter, or any personal wrong, however hideous the sin, would be an offence the more. He stood by almost stupidly while the young priest, with his keen, clear-cut, Churchman-like face, put on his surplice and prepared himself for the ceremony; then, with a sinking of heart beyond description, followed him up the narrow wooden stairs, which creaked at every step. He said to himself that this was the fiend endowed with every virtue who had put it in the woman's head to drag him to his undoing; but so miserable was he that he felt no anger, no resentment against the meddling priest, as men are so apt to do. He recognised that it was no doubt his nature, that he thought it his duty; that to this man he himself was a vile seducer, and that the poor victim upstairs was the confiding, loving girl, whose fame had been ruined and her heart broken! These thoughts were so strangely out of keeping with the facts, and he regarded them with such a dazed impartiality, that when he entered the room in which this dreadful ceremony was to take place, there was a smile upon his lips. But the smile was soon driven away by the sight which now met his eyes. In the soft suffusion of the daylight the dying woman was scarcely so ghastly as by the light of the candle on the night before, but the spectacle she presented was more dreadful than anything that Oliver had been able to conceive. The decorations of a bride dressed for her wedding, or, rather, a

45

hideous travesty of those decorations, surrounded the worn and sunken face. Some dreadful artificial flowers—orange blossom, of all things in the world! no idea of the meaning of it being in their minds, but only a grotesque acquaintance with its general use at weddings—were placed in a bristling wreath about her head. The pink ribbon was withdrawn, and bows of ghostly white placed at her throat and hands; and over all there was thrown a veil costly worked with huge flowers, through which the gleaming eyes, the mouth distended with its ghastly smile, showed like a living death.

A cry of horror burst from Oliver in spite of himself; and even the rigid priest was moved.

'Why did you do her up like that?' he said, in a sharp tone to Matilda, who stood admiring her handiwork.

The poor creature herself had a look of delighted vanity in her terrible gleaming eyes. The mother had a mirror in her hands, in which she had been displaying her own appearance to the bride. The bride! Oliver turned away and hid his face in his hands.

'I cannot—I cannot carry out this farce,' he said.

The curate placed his hand upon Wentworth's arm. 'You must,' he said, with his severe, unpitying voice. 'Whose fault is it that this is a farce? Stand forward, sir, and give this poor wreck, this creature you have ruined, what compensation you can at the last.'

Oliver raised his eyes to his uncompromising judge with a wonder which paralysed all effort. 'You are mistaken,' he said:

but to pause now was impossible; he went forward doggedly and placed himself by the bed, and listened with a dull horror, as under a spell, to those words—those words which he had thought of under so different a meaning—words of solemn joy and devotion, words that could only be endured for the sake of the pledge they sanctified. He listened and he took his part like a man in a dream. He had provided no ring, and the ceremony was interrupted till an old, shabby little trinket, set with some discoloured turquoises, was hunted up from a drawer. But it was completed at last, and she was his wife—his wife! She put back the veil with a nervous movement, and inclined her head towards his. Was that necessary, too? Was there to be no end to these exactions? 'Oliver!' she cried.

He turned from her, sick to the heart. 'Take those fooleries away—don't you see how horrible it is?' he said to Matilda, and hurried downstairs, flying from the look and the touch of the woman who—oh, Heaven!—was now his wife.

The little priest followed him. He was as severe as ever. 'You have done something in the way of atonement,' he said, 'but if this is how you are to follow it up, I warn you that such an atonement will not be accepted. It must be from the heart.'

Oliver turned upon him. He seemed to be coming to life again after the dismal paralytic fit through which he had passed.

'Did it ever happen to you,' he said, 'to make a mistake?'

The clergyman had begun to take off his surplice. He turned round in the act, and looked at Wentworth. But the question did not daunt him as it would have daunted many men, 'Possibly,' he replied, 'but very seldom, as a man. In discharge of my office I make no mistakes.'

'You have made one now,' said the bridegroom. 'Oh, I do not excuse myself. I know well enough how hideous, how paltry, how miserable it is:—but it was not for me to make atonement. I was no deceiver, no seducer—'

'You are a man of education and intelligence,' said the other in his keen, clear tones, 'and that was an ignorant, foolish girl. Is that not enough—did you ever meet on equal terms? And now you are not on equal terms, for you are well and strong and she is dying—perhaps with only a few hours to live.'

Oliver drew back without a word. It was the argument that had moved him at first, which he had found irresistible. He at the height of happiness, and she dying: but he was not at the height of happiness now. A more miserable man could not be. How was he to explain this day's work when all was over, when he was free? Was it possible that Grace would understand him, that she would still accept his hand which had been pledged under such different circumstances, which had been given away from her to another, and such another! He could not go back into the room where it had been done, or see the poor creature who was his bride with all that dismal paraphernalia about her. He went out and walked and walked till his limbs trembled under him. Then he remembered that he had not eaten anything that day. By this time it was afternoon, darkening towards evening, still drizzling, wet and miserable. He got himself some food, a kind of hasty dinner, in the first tavern he came to. And then, strengthened a little and calmed, went back. Perhaps, dreadful hope, it might be all over by the time he had traversed the many streets and had reached again that miserable place of fate.

CHAPTER VI

It was a dreadful hope to lie down with at night, and rise up with in the morning—that morning or night might bring him a message to say that all was over, and that he was free. But it was still more dreadful that this message never came. When he saw her next she had rallied, rallied amazingly, the doctor said; but he added that it was only a flicker in the socket—only a question of time—a day or two, perhaps an hour or two. Oliver had revulsions of pity, attended with a loathing which he could scarcely keep under. He had to suffer himself to be drawn towards her, to feel his neck encircled by her arms, to kiss her cheek, to listen to her as long as he could bear it, while she told him how often she had thought of him; how she had never loved any man but he, how she had felt that she could not die in peace till she had seen him again. It required all his pity for her to strengthen him for these confessions, to enable him to meet that meretricious smile, those ghastly little tricks of fascination which he could remember to have laughed at even in other times. How horrible they were to him now no words could say. He went through the same miserable streets daily till he shuddered at his own errand and at the dreadful hope that was always in his heart in spite of himself, the hope that he might hear that all was over. His mind revolted from his fate with a self-indignation and rage against all that had brought it about, against the wrong done to the most miserable of human creatures by wishing her death, and at himself for the weakness which had brought him into this strait. To live with no desire so strong in him as that this poor girl should die, to make his way to the poor little house that sheltered her day by day, sick with hope that he might hear she was dead—oh! what was this but murder—murder never coming to any execution, but involved in every thought? But afterwards there came upon this unhappy man something more dreadful still, the moment in which a new thought sprang up in him—the thought that it was never to be over, that she was not going to die, that the flicker in the socket of which the doctor had spoken was the filling in of oil to the flame, the rising of new force and life. When this thought came to him, what with the horror of the possibility, and the horror of knowing that he grudged that possibility, and would take life from her if he could, Oliver's cup seemed full, despair took possession of him. Everything grew dark in heaven and earth. She was going to live, not to die; and what, oh! what, most miserable of men, was he to do?

The first thing that enlightened him was a change in her phrases when she talked to him of her own devotion, of her longings after him.

'I knew as it would give me a chance for my life if I could see you once again.'

51

It had been at first only to die in peace after she had seen him that she proposed. And when his eyes, quickened with this horrible light, began to observe closely, he perceived that she spoke more strongly, that her emaciation was not so great nor her breathing so difficult. She was going to live, not die; and what was to become of him? What was he to do?

All this time—and it went on, gliding day after day, and week after week, he scarcely could tell how—he was receiving letters and calls back, and anxious inquiries and appeals from those he had left behind. Grace wrote to him—first a letter of simple love and anxiety, hoping his friend was better, anticipating news from him; then more serious, fearing that the illness was grave indeed, that he was absorbed in nursing, but begging for a word; then anxious, alarmed lest something should have happened to him; then with an outburst of feeling, entreating to know what it meant, imploring him only to tell her there was a reason, even if he could not say what that reason was. Then silence. But even this lasted but for a few days. She wrote again to say that she could not believe he had changed, that it was to her incredible; but should it be so, imploring to know from himself that so it was. The dignity and the tenderness, and the high trust and honour which would not permit any pettiness of offence, went to his very heart. He sent her a few miserable lines in reply, imploring her to wait. 'Some of my sins have found me out,' he said; 'the sins I acknowledged to you. But oh! for the love of God, do not abandon me, for then I shall lose my last hope.'

He got from her in return these words, and no more, 'I will never abandon you unless I have it from your own hand that I must.' And then no other word.

52

But Trix plied him with a thousand. What did he mean flying like this from his betrothed and his family and all his prospects? What did he mean, what was his reason, what in the name of all that was foolish was he thinking of? Did he mean to break his word, to give up his engagement, to break all their hearts? What was it? What was it? What was it?

He left her letters at last unopened. He could make no answer to them. He could give no explanation. Every day he had hoped that perhaps—perhaps. And now that his horror had come over him he was less disposed to write than ever. If it should be as, God forgive him, he feared, what was there in store for him? What should he do? The veins of his eyeballs seemed to fill with blood, and the air grew dark in his sight; a blank, sinking void opened before him; he could perceive only that he must be swallowed up in it, swept beyond sight and knowledge; but for the others who loved him, he did not know how to reveal to them the terrible cause.

During all this time of suspense he was very kind to the woman to whom he had linked himself like the living to the dead. He got her everything she wished for—delicate food, fine wine, all that could afford a little ease to her body or amusement to her mind. Such forms of kindness are appreciated in regions where life is more practical than sentimental. The mother and sister sang his praises. 'Die! no, he don't want you to die,' they said. 'What would he send you all these nice things for, and feed you up, and get you that water-bed that cost such a deal of money, if he wanted you to die? But you're that exacting now you're Mrs. Wentworth.'

'I am Mrs. Wentworth: that's one thing none can take from me,' she said.

He heard her as he came up the narrow stair, trying as no one else did to make as little noise as possible, and that wave of loathing which sickened his very soul came over him. How horrible it all was, incredible, impossible, that she should bear that name! that it should be bandied about in a place like this— his mother's name, his wife's. Ah! but she, and no other, was his wife. This was the evening when she said to him, 'I feel I am really getting better, Oliver. I believe I'll cheat the doctors yet: and it will all be your doing, dear. You'll take me abroad, and my lungs will come right, and we shall be as happy as the day is long.'

He made no reply, but avoided the hand with which she tried to draw him to her, and asked a few questions of her mother, before he bade her good night. He met the doctor as he was going downstairs, and waited to hear his bulletin. The parish doctor had found his manners, which had only been put aside when there was no need for such vanities: but he was not used to fine words. He said,—

'That wife of yours is a wonderful woman; it seems as if it might be possible to pull her through after all. She has such pluck and spirit, and that's half the battle.'

'You told me,' said Wentworth, with a sternness which was almost threatening, 'that there was no hope of recovery.'

'You don't seem best pleased with my good news,' said the doctor, with a laugh. 'As for hope of recovery, there wasn't a scrap in her then state. And her life isn't worth a pinch of snuff even now; but with a husband that can take her abroad to a warm climate and give her every luxury, why, there is hope for any woman; and I can but say I think it possible that she may pull through. That should be good news for you—but perhaps unexpected,' he said, with a keen glance.

Wentworth made no reply. He bowed his head slightly, and went out before the doctor, walking out into the darkness and distance with a straight, unobservant abstraction. He never looked to right or left; and went out of his way for nothing, as if he saw nothing in his way. The doctor looking after him observed this idly, as people observe things that don't concern them. He thought that on the whole it was a very curious incident. He could not think of any motive that could have brought about such a marriage. He wondered a little what the man could be thinking of to do such a thing: a woman who had long lost any signs of prettiness, if she had ever possessed any; poor, uneducated, and of damaged character. Why had he married her? and, having married her, was he disappointed that she did not die? He stood and watched Wentworth till he was out of sight, saying to himself that he should not be surprised if that man were found in the river or on Hampstead Heath some of these days. But it was no concern of his.

Oliver went home to his chambers, walking all the way. It was a very long way, and when he got there he was very tired, very tired and sick to death. He ate a mouthful of the dinner provided for him, and drank a glass or two of wine, dully, silently, keeping his thoughts, as it were, at bay, not allowing himself to indulge in them. Afterwards he sat down at his writing-table, and wrote a long, a very long letter, which he closed and sealed, getting up to get matches to light his taper, and searching in every corner he could think of for the sealing-wax; though why he should seal it he could not have explained. It was a mark of special solemnity, in keeping with the great crisis and the state of mind in which he was. Afterwards he sat down and thought long and very gravely. He went over the position in every possible point of view. There could not be a more hopeless one. Betrothed to a woman he loved and approved with every faculty of his being, yet married to one whom he did not pretend to love for whom, at the best, he had no feeling above pity—and at the worst—There began to penetrate into his brain, unused to such thoughts, a dull suspicion that he might have been all through the victim of a cheat; but it did not make much difference, and he felt no resentment, nothing but a profound sensation of hopelessness, past help or care. Whether it was deception all through, or whether it was the judgment of God upon him, who had sinned and had not suffered, and had been on the edge of winning, he so unworthy, the best that man can have in this world—it did not seem to matter much. In either case the result was the same—that here he stood with life made impossible to him, with a blank wall before him, and nothing to be done, no way of deliverance nor even of escape. He looked out in that curious blank way over the future, asking himself what it would be his duty to do. It would be his duty to take her away to a warm country, as her doctor had said—to give her all the care that she required, 'every luxury'—these were the words—and so ensure her recovery. To do anything else would be inhuman. And as for Grace—ah, for Grace! To him she must henceforth be a sacred thing apart. He must not see her, speak to her, lean his heart upon her evermore. That was all ended—ended and over. He had written a long letter to his brother-in-law, telling him all the circumstances. He was not a man who could go on with deceits and false positions, trying miserably to stand between one and another. He might have done that, perhaps, for a time, might have beguiled Grace with letters, and explained by any false excuse his detention in London, his absence from her—but to what good? One day or other it would all have to be disclosed, now that it was evident that this woman was not going to die; however long he might fight it off, the necessity would come at last. And it was better that she should know now, than only at the moment when he should be leaving England with his wife. His wife! Oh, terrible word! Oh, awful, impossible fate!

This sudden realisation of what was before him made his mind start like a restive horse, and he found himself once more before that blank wall. It would be his duty to do it, and he could not do it. He did not trifle with himself nor elude this question any more than he would deceive the woman he loved. He looked out upon what was before him, and he said to himself that he could not do it—he could not pretend to do it. Other men might have the courage to struggle, but not he. There was only the coward's remedy remaining to him, only the base man's way—to turn and flee. He had written it all in his letter to Ford, although it seemed to him that when he wrote that letter he had not so clearly perceived that there was only one thing to do. He had bidden his brother-in-law to secure a living somehow for this wretched creature who bore his name, to use the little he would leave for her, and to eke it out—or finally, with the boldness of a man whom earthly motives had ceased to sway, to put this last inconceivable legacy into the hands of Grace.

'I know she will do it,' he had said.

He knew she would do it, God bless her! She would understand why of all terrible things he dared to ask that of her; and she would do it. That was all there could be to arrange before—

Oliver was not of that mind that is the mode of the present moment. He was no doubter. He believed in the canon 'gainst self-slaughter, as well as in righteousness and judgment to come; but there is something in the unutterable sensations with which a man finds himself thus placed before evils which are too many for him, driven to the last extremity, and unable to move one way or other, which works a strange change upon the mind on this as on other matters of faith. When we are doing any act in our own person, it seems so much less strange to us, so much more natural, than when we contemplate it from the point of view of another man. He did not think either of the sin or of the cowardice. He thought only of the last resort, the last way of escape from that which was intolerable, which was more than man could bear. To describe the way by which a man comes to this point, to entertain the idea of ending his own life, is impossible. Those who are brought so far seldom survive to tell how it has been. It seemed to Oliver something like the arising and going to the Father of the prodigal. God, it seemed to him, would understand it all; the confusion in his soul, the intolerableness, the impossibility. If anyone else misunderstood, God would understand; and as for the punishment that might follow, he thought that he could take that like a man. No punishment could be equal to this. He would say that he did not mean to avoid punishment, that he was ready for anything, only not this; not the ghastly life which was insupportable, not the falsehood, not the treachery. Suffering, honest suffering—yes!—torments if God thought it worth the trouble—anything except this, which was more than he could bear. His mind was all wrong, confused, stupefied with all that had happened to him, and with the turning upside down of all his purposes, and the bitter ending to what had been a good impulse, surely a good impulse, an impulse of pity without consideration of himself; also with the wretched state in which he had been living, the want of food, the want of sleep, the sense of treachery to all he loved, the union to all he loathed; it was all intolerable, insupportable, turning his brain.

He had a pair of pistols in his room—pretty toys, decorated with silver, wrought in delicate designs—which someone had given to him. He took them down and opened the box and examined them curiously to see how they worked and that all was in order. He looked at the little bullet which could do so much, and weighed it in his hand with a dazed smile, and a kind of strange amusement. So little—and yet in it lay that for which not all the wealth of the world could find an antidote. He charged both weapons with a smile at himself for that too, thinking how very unlikely it was that the two would be wanted, and feeling almost something of the pleasure with which a boy prepares for his first shot, with a half horror, half delight. And then he thought how it would be best to do it. He did not want to disfigure himself unnecessarily, to go through all eternity with a bound-up jaw, like—who was it? Robespierre. This brought a sort of smile upon his face; he knew that it was folly to think of Robespierre; for all eternity—with his face bound up! and yet it amused him to think of the awful, grotesque figure, and to determine that he should not be like that. The temple or behind the ear; that was the better way; and then there would be no disfigurement. The hair would hide it, and Grace would see him and not be horrified—not horrified—only perhaps broken-hearted. But that had to be, any way.

Would he hear the report as sound travels before his senses were all stilled? He heard something, a jar and tinkle, which made him start at the very moment he felt that cold mouth of death. The touch of the pistol and then a jerk of his arm and a clanging world of sound, and then—no more. It disturbed his arm and the steadiness of his touch; and the report followed harmlessly, the bullet going somewhere, he knew not where, leaving him sitting there with the jar of the concussion in the finger which had pulled that trigger. The sound seemed to wake him up like a clap of thunder. He sprang to his feet, flinging the little weapon away with a burning sense of despising himself, of scorn for his intention, scorn for his failure. Was he a coward too, doubly a coward, ready to run away, yet weak enough to be stopped in the act? A sudden heat of shame came over him; he burst into a laugh of scorn, self-ridicule, derision—God in heaven! had he been frightened at the last moment? by what, by his nerves, by a fancied sound, like a child?

What? what? a fancied sound? No; but the commonest, most vulgar noise in the world: the bell at his door, pealing, tingling, jarring, with a repeated and violent summons into the silence of the night.

CHAPTER VII

They had all been disturbed by it beyond expression; by his absence, by his silence, his sudden, strange departure which, natural enough at the minute, appeared now, in the light of subsequent events, so extraordinary, which now looked like a flight, but—from what? From happiness, from well-being, from everything that the heart of man could desire. Mr. Ford was a person of a very sturdy mind, not given to fancies like his wife, but after a fortnight had passed he was almost more anxious than she was. He questioned her closely as to Oliver's past life. Had she ever heard of any entanglement?

'There must be some one who has a claim upon him, who would expose him to Grace, if not worse,' he said; at which Trix was naturally indignant.

'You men have such bad imaginations,' she cried. 'How should he have any entanglements? He has been fond of Grace since— since—'

'Since he saw her here six months ago, Trix.'

Trix grew very red, and the tears came into her eyes. 'You mean, Tom, that Oliver, that—that my brother got fond of Grace only when—'

'I don't mean anything of the sort,' said Tom Ford, 'it is women who have bad imaginations, though, perhaps, in a different way. I mean that he had forgotten all about her. But when he saw her again, and saw how nice she was—for she is a very nice woman, poor thing! far too nice to be made a wreck of for the sake of some baggage—'

'Tom! you have taken leave of your senses, I think.'

'My dear, you know well enough, just as well as I do, that Oliver hasn't been immaculate. But why the deuce didn't he have the courage to tell the truth? Why didn't he speak to you, or me, if it comes to that? If he had made a clean breast of it—'

'We don't know yet that there is anything to make a clean breast of,' said Trix, beginning to cry. And she put on her bonnet in a disturbed way and went over to Grace for comfort, who might be supposed to want comfort more than she did. Grace was very pale, but composed, and met her friend with a smile.

'I don't know anything,' she said, 'but he asks me to wait, and I mean to wait. Why should we condemn him? There must be a reason, and when he can he will tell us. It is not out of mere wantonness he is staying away.'

They had all given up tacitly the pretence about the sick friend.

63

That had been dismissed at a quite early date; the reality that was in it being beyond any guesses they could make.

'Oh, Grace, you are the best of us all! You are the one that is the worst treated, and you are the most kind.'

'Trix, we don't know that there is any ill-treatment at all,' said Grace. She was very subdued, very pale. It almost overcame her composure altogether when a servant came in with a large packet, one of the many wedding presents that were arriving daily. 'I have not the heart to open them,' she said, leaning her head upon Trix's shoulder, who flew to her with instant comprehension: 'and yet I want to open them that nobody may suppose—Look,' she said, pointing to a table covered with glittering spoils. 'Look at all that, and the congratulations that come with them. And to think that I don't know, I don't know even—'

'Oh, Grace, all will be well, all will be well! long before that.'

Grace did not say anything, but she shook her head. 'He does not even say that all will be well; he says only—wait. But I will wait,' she said, composing herself. Trix did not get much comfort out of this visit. She went home indignant, angry beyond telling with her brother, though she could not bear that her husband should give utterance and emphasis to her fears. And for some days after the talk of those two people was of nothing but Oliver and what his meaning could be. Mrs. Ford sent off a long and eloquent letter to him the night after these discussions, but received no answer to that any more than to her former letters. And Ford, too, wrote one, which was very much more serious.

64

Ford, who never wrote a letter except on business, leaving everything else to his wife. Ford put before his brother-in-law indeed the business view of the matter. He had come under certain engagements, did he intend or not to fulfil them? He told Oliver that his conduct was mere madness, that it was against all his interests, that he was destroying his own credit and cutting his own throat. What did he mean by it? but adding that whatever he meant, which was his own concern, he ought not to lose a moment in coming back, and doing what he could to repair the fearful mistake he was making. The letter was curt and business-like, but very much in earnest. Oliver had come by that time to a condition of mind in which arguments of that or any other kind were of no avail. He never read this letter; did he not know everything that could be said to him? had he not said it all and twenty times more to himself?

After this appeal, however, and that much more eloquent, certainly more lengthy, one of Trix's, silence fell again, and the days so anxiously watched at every post for letters passed on and brought nothing. The excitement, the tension, the fear of suspense grew hourly. As yet they had managed to keep it to themselves. Nobody knew, unless it might be the servants, who know everything. Grace was the best in this effort; she replied with so composed a look, so steady a smile to the many curious questions addressed to her as to Mr. Wentworth's long absence, that curiosity was baffled. Trix did not know how she could do it. She herself grew red, the tears came to her eyes when she was questioned, in spite of herself. It was always on the cards that she might break down altogether, and take some sympathetic visitor into her confidence. She was like her brother, not of so

65

steady a soul as Grace, and this was to her insupportable, as his more terrible anguish was to him.

It was from Tom Ford, however, the man without nerves, the cool-headed, mercantile person whom Trix had so often stormed at as unsensitive and hard to move, that the touch of impatience came. He said one day at breakfast suddenly, without warning, 'I think, Trix, if there is no word to-day, I shall run up to town and see with my own eyes what Oliver is up to. We cannot let this go on.'

'Run up to town to-day? Tom, you have heard something; you know more than we do—'

'Nothing of the sort: but I feel a responsibility. He is your brother, and that poor girl met him in our house. I must see what it means. I can't let it run on like this. She has no brother to stand up for her. I want to know what the fellow means.'

'Tom, you must not go and bully Oliver. He would never stand that, even when he was a boy.'

'I have no intention of bullying him. I want to know what he means,' Mr. Ford repeated doggedly. And then Trix, what with fear lest his interference should be resented, what with eagerness to solve the mystery, insisted on going too; to which her husband did not object, having foreseen it. She went out immediately and told Grace. The sense of being about to do something is a great matter to a woman who in most emergencies of her life is compelled to wait while others do what is to be done. Action restores trust to her, and a sense that all must come right.

'Tom and I are going. Tom has business of his own, and he takes this opportunity: and he thinks I may as well go too, and then this mystery will be cleared up. I shall telegraph to you at once, the moment I have seen him, Grace.'

Grace was greatly startled by this sudden resolution, though she said very little. But when they started by the afternoon train, she was there at the station to meet them.

'I think I will go, too,' she said. 'You know I have a great deal of—shopping to do.' And not a word was said by which a stranger could have divined that this was an expedition, not of shopping, but of outraged love and despair. They arrived late with a sort of understanding that nothing could be done that night. But when the ladies had been settled in their hotel, Mr. Ford went out to take, as he said, a walk. He went through the gloomy streets; through the Strand, with all its noise and crowd, to the Temple, where Oliver's chambers were. He had not told his wife even where he was going. He thought there might be something to learn which it would be better these women should not hear; and perhaps he thought, too, that it would be a triumph, without their aid, to lead the wanderer back. He went all that long way on foot, thinking within himself that the later he was the more likely he was to find Oliver, and turning over in his mind what he should say. He would represent to him the folly of his behaviour, the madness of throwing thus his best hopes away. Ford was very anxious, more anxious than he would have confessed to anyone. He did not, indeed, think of such a possibility as that which had really happened; but his mind was prepared for some complication, some entanglement

67

that had to be got rid of; perhaps even some tie made in earlier years which Oliver believed himself to have got rid of, and which had come to life again, as such things will. Who could tell? He might have married and have thought his wife was dead, and have been roused out of his happiness by the terrible news that this was not true. Such a thing is not uncommon in fiction, for instance; and Mr. Ford, like many busy men, was a great novel reader. He was ready even, terrible though it would be, to hear that this was the cause of his brother-in-law's disappearance. But, perhaps, he hoped, it might be something not so bad as that.

He was a long time gone, so long, that Trix got alarmed, and in her uneasiness burst into Grace's room, who was going to rest, to wait with what patience she might for the morning, which, she said to herself, must end all suspense. Her self-restraint was sadly broken by the irruption into her room of Trix in all her fever of alarm.

'Where do you think he can have gone? Oh, what do you think can have happened to him?—such dreadful things happen in London,' Mrs. Ford cried, rising gradually into higher and higher excitement. She thought of garroters; of roughs who might have followed him along the Embankment (though she scarcely knew where that was), and already her imagination figured him lying on the pavement senseless, perhaps unconscious, unable to tell anyone where to carry him.

'The only address that would be found upon him would be our address at home, and if they telegraphed there, and then telegraphed here, how much time must be lost? And it is too late even to telegraph,' she cried, as these miserable anticipations gained upon her. But what could two women do in a London hotel? They could not go out with a lantern and search for his body about the streets, and they did not even know where or in what direction he had gone. 'He has gone to find your brother,' Grace suggested once; but Trix would not hear of this. 'Never,' she said, 'without letting me know.'

At last, when it was long past midnight, a hansom drove up to the hotel, and Mr. Ford appeared, exceedingly pale and with an air of great agitation and distress. He told them that Oliver had been very ill: that he would have to leave England, to get into a milder climate. He would not be more explicit; a milder climate and to get out of England, that was all he would say. He had a letter in his hand which he had been reading as best he could by the lamplight as he drove back, and by the dying candles in Wentworth's room, into which he had forced his way. He told his wife as soon as they were alone that he had found on Oliver's desk this long letter addressed to himself, and gave her an outline of the story, which brought out such a shriek from Trix, as sounded through the partition and startled Grace once more in the solitude of her room, to which she had returned. She appeared between the husband and wife a minute after in her white dressing gown, white as the gown she wore.

'There is something you have not told me. Tell me what it is,' she said. It had been a momentary relief to her to know that Oliver was ill. If that was so, everything might be explained; but—And now she heard that there was something more.

'Oh, Grace, go to bed; oh, go to bed. We don't know ourselves

69

yet. To-morrow morning, the very first thing, after you have had a night's rest—'

'I cannot rest to-night,' she said, with parched lips, 'until I know. There is nothing that cannot be borne,' she added, a moment afterwards, 'except not to know.'

They made a curious contrast. Trix all flushed with excitement and distress, her voice choked with tears, her eyes overflowing; and she who was even more concerned, she who believed herself to be Oliver Wentworth's bride, in that breathless silence of suspense, afraid to make a sound, to waste a word, lest perhaps she should miss some recollection, some indication of what to her was life or death.

'I have something here to read, if you think you can bear it. It is not good news.'

'Oh, Tom, for the love of Heaven, don't! Grace, go to your room, dear! Oh, go to bed, and I'll come—I'll come and tell you as soon as we know.'

'It is Oliver's hand,' said Grace. 'I can bear whatever he has written. But let me hear it at once, for this suspense is more than I can bear.'

'Grace—Grace!—'

But Mr. Ford interrupted his wife. He saw that Grace was not to be put off any longer, and indeed was capable of nothing but knowing the truth. He brought the easiest chair for her, with that pathetic instinct which makes us so careful of the bodies of those whose hearts we are about to crush. She made no opposition.

70

She would have done anything—anything, so long as it brought her nearer the end. Ford had the discrimination to see this, and that the only thing she could not bear was delay. He began at once to read the letter, of which he had already told the chief facts to his wife. The two candles flickered, placed together on the mantelpiece, and drearily doubled in the mirror behind, while the bare hotel room, with its big bed and wardrobes, formed an indistinct, cold background. Mr. Ford stood by the mantelpiece, and read slowly, in a voice of which he had not always command. Trix behind him, sobbing, crying, exclaiming, unable to restrain herself, moved up and down, sometimes stopping to look over his shoulder, sometimes throwing for a moment herself into a seat. In the centre, the white figure of Grace, all white, motionless, sat rigid, scarcely breathing. Grace was prepared for everything. Except a start and shiver when she heard of the marriage, she scarcely made a sign from beginning to end. The others were distracted, even in their own horror and pity, by an anxious desire to know how she would take it. But Grace was disturbed by no such secondary feelings. At that point her hands, which had been lying in her lap, closed in a convulsive clasp, but save this she made no sign, listening to every word till the end. Even after the end, it was some time before she moved or spoke. Then she pointed to it, and said faintly, 'It is a letter—is he—has he gone away?'

'You have heard all this. I must tell you more—I must tell you all I know,' said Ford. He was much agitated, his lips quivering, his voice now and then failing altogether. 'I believe,' he said, struggling to get out the words, 'that the noise I made at his door saved his life, that he had thought for a moment of putting an end to everything; there was a pistol on the floor.'

71

She rose to her feet with a quick, sudden cry, 'That! That!' and clutched for support at the mantelpiece, against which Mr. Ford was leaning, and where there seemed to rise in the mirror a pale, white ghost, facing the darker figure.

'Oliver,' she cried, 'Oliver! tell me everything. That is his last word, and he is dead!'

'No, no, no—oh, no!' came in Trix's voice from behind.

Ford took her hands from their clutch on the marble, and put her back into her chair. All he was afraid of was that she might faint, or die, perhaps, in their hands.

'He is not dead, so far as I know. He has gone away. How could he meet you? Oh, Grace, what can we say to you, Trix and I? It is our fault! My poor girl, cry or something. Don't look like that. You must put him out of your thoughts.'

She shook herself free of him with impatience. 'I am asking you about Oliver,' she said. 'Oliver! Where is he? Have you left him, with no one near him, no one to comfort him? Trix, are you going to him, or shall I?'

The husband and wife looked at each other in dismay. Mrs. Ford stilled in a moment her sobs and exclamations, not knowing what to reply.

'You are nearest him in blood, but I am nearest in—' Grace paused for a moment. 'He will want to know that I—understand,' she said slowly, as if speaking to herself.

'He has no right to know anything about you,' Ford said

72

roughly, in the agitation of his mind. 'You must think no more of him, Grace. He has no claim upon you. This miserable marriage—'

'Marriage,' she said, again rising, resisting his attempt to support her. 'You think a woman has no idea but marriage. What is that to me? I have been fearing I knew not what—and now my mind is relieved, I understand. It is not that I forgive him,' she added, after a moment, with an indescribable look of tender pride and dignity, 'I approve. You may blame him if you will—I approve. And if he should die, I accept his legacy. I thank God he had that trust in me, and that he did what was right. Though it should kill us both, what does that matter? He has done only what was right, and I approve!'

CHAPTER VIII

This was how she took it, as the young priest had taken it, as an atonement, as a duty. Instead of the despair they had expected, she was excited and inspired as people are who die for a great cause. She did not and would not take into account all that made Oliver's strange sacrifice a thing without justice, without dignity—a mere hideous postscript to a mere vulgar sin, repented of indeed, but not made less vulgar and hideous even by repentance. Fortunately for Grace, nothing of this entered her mind. He had made atonement, he had righted a wrong at the cost of his own happiness. To be sure, it was at the cost of hers also, but in her exaltation she never thought of that. What she did mourn over was that he should not have told her; that he had suffered bitterly and cruelly, and had been driven to the uttermost despair rather than tell her; that he should have thought her incapable of the same sacrifice as he was making, less noble than himself. This hurt her in passing, but she had not time to think more of it. In the meantime he must be comforted, reassured, cared for. He must know that she understood him, that she—yes, she who was the victim, who had to bear the penalty—approved. She was inspired with strength and courage to do this. She was no victim—she was a martyr, sharing his martyrdom for the sake of what was right.

I need scarcely say that the Fords no more understood her than if she had been speaking a foreign language. They gazed at her with horror and bewilderment. They asked each other, had she not loved him after all? That a woman who loved him could have so accepted this revelation was to them incredible. Mr. Ford was almost angry with her in the disappointment with which he saw this extraordinary and un-looked-for effect. He said stiffly, that he was very glad that she could take it so philosophically—more than poor Oliver had done—but that as for comforting or helping him that was impossible. For Oliver had disappeared, and, so far as was known, might be heard of no more. How he had got out of his chambers, his anxious brother-in-law did not know; he supposed it must have been at the moment when, receiving no answer to his summons, he had gone to seek for help to break open the door. On his return the door had been found open, the rooms empty, the letter on the table, the pistol lying on the floor; but of Oliver no sign; and that was all that anyone knew.

It was evident, at least, that nothing could be done till next day. And Grace withdrew from the troubled pair, who did not understand her any more than they knew how to deal with the horrible crisis altogether. She went slowly, steadily to her own room, not trembling and sick at heart as when she had come.

The suspense was over—now she knew everything. Her heart was in so strange an exaltation, that for the moment she seemed to feel no pain. It seemed to her as if Oliver and she were martyrs about to come out upon some scaffold hand in hand, and for the righting of wrong and the redeeming of the lost to die. Such a crisis has an intoxication peculiar to itself. She did not sleep all night, but lay down and thought over everything. The worst was that he had not told her. If he had but trusted in her, it was she who should have stood by him all along, and taken his part and justified him before the world.

She met Mrs. Ford in the morning as she left her room, putting a stop to all those attempts to make an invalid of her, and treat her as if she were ill, which is the common expedient of the lookers-on in cases of grief or mental suffering. Her face was pale but not without colour, very clear, like a sky after rain; the eyes limpid and large, as if they had increased in size somehow during the night.

'When you have had your breakfast,' she said, with a smile,—'I have ordered it for you—then there are several things I wish you to do—for me—'

'Grace!' Mrs. Ford was astonished by her look, and felt herself taken by surprise. 'You—you don't mean—shopping?' she asked, almost mysteriously, confounded by her friend's calm.

Grace gave her a reproachful look. 'I have ordered a carriage, too,' she said, taking no notice of the suggestion. 'Tell me when you are ready.'

Mrs. Ford, looking with guilty countenance at her watch, went quickly to the table at which her husband was seated, eating a hurried, but not at all an insufficient, breakfast.

'I don't know what she means,' Mr. Ford said. 'She has ordered a feast. There's half a dozen things. No, no more; don't bring any more. Trix, I'm going off to the Temple, of course, at once, and if I can find out anything or get any trace of where he has gone, I'll telegraph. Mind what I told you last night. You must try and get her sent home.'

'She is going to do her—shopping,' said Trix. To tell the truth, she did not herself believe this, but it was the first thing that occurred to her to say.

'Her SHOPPING!' Mr. Ford panted forth, with a great burst of agitated laughter. 'Great Heavens, you don't say so! Her shopping! What a fool I have been to put myself out about her. You women will do your shopping on the Day of Judgment.'

Trix thought it was perhaps better to let him go away with this idea; it would leave him, she felt, more free. And when Grace joined her with her bonnet on, and disclosed her design, Mrs. Ford was startled for the moment, but yielded without much difficulty. They drove away in the soft morning, when even the London streets look like spring, miles away through the interminable streets, until at last they came to that one among so many others where the pavement was worn by Oliver's weary feet, where he had gone with his heart bleeding, so that it was strange he had left no trace. It seemed to both the women as if he had left traces of these painful steps, as if the sky darkened when they got there, and the air began to moan with coming storm. It did so, it was true, but not because of Oliver. A sudden April shower (though it was in May) fell in a quick discharge of glittering drops as they drove up to the house. Not to the door — for already a cab was standing which blocked the way: but the cab was not all. A little crowd, excited and tumultuous, had gathered round the steps, some pushing in to the very threshold of the open door. It did not seem wonderful to the ladies that the crowd should be here. It seemed of a piece with all the rest. A thing so extraordinary and out of nature had happened, it was nothing strange if the common people about raised a wonder over it, as everyone who knew must do. They forgot that this affair was interesting only to themselves, and that nobody here was aware of their existence. They made their way with heavy hearts to the edge of the crowd.

'Is there anything wrong? What is the matter?' Trix asked of one of the throng.

'They say as she's dying, ma'am,' said the woman to whom she spoke.

'Ah, poor thing!' cried another, anxious to give information. The crowd turned its attention at once to the two ladies.

'Just a-going to take her first drive out,' said one. 'All in the grand fur cloak he gave her.'

'A man as grudged her nothing.'

'It's like on the stage,' said another. 'Ladies, a rich gentleman, and grudged her nothing. And she's never got time to enjoy it. Oh, she's never got time to enjoy it!'

These voices ran altogether, confusing each other. They conveyed little meaning to the minds of the two ladies, who heard imperfectly, and did not understand.

Grace was the one who pushed through the crowd. 'Let us pass, please. We have come to see someone,' she said, clutching Trix's dress with her hand.

'Oh, is that the doctor? Stand back and let the doctor pass,' said a voice from within the door of the little parlour. The speaker came out as she spoke. She was the mother, with a pale and frightened face surmounted by a bonnet gay with ribbons and flowers. 'Oh, ladies, I cannot speak to you now! Oh, if it's anything about the dressmaking, Matilda will come to you to-morrow. We're in great trouble now. Oh, doctor, doctor, here you are at last!'

Then a man brushed past, hurrying in. Grace followed, not knowing what she did. She never forgot the scene she saw. In an arm-chair, the only one in the room, sat propped up a young woman wrapped in a fur cloak, with a white bonnet covered with flowers. Her eyes were half open; her jaws had dropped. Another young woman, apparently her sister, stood stroking her softly, calling to her: 'Oh, wake up, Ally!—oh, wake up!—there's the carriage at the door, and here—here's the doctor come to see you.' Through the sound of this frightened, half-weeping voice came the sharp, clear tones of the doctor: 'How long has she been like this? Lay her down—lay her down anywhere. Yes, on the floor, if there's nowhere else. Silence, silence, woman! Can't you see—'

There was an interval of quiet, and then the voice of the mother,

'I'll get a mattress in a moment. She can't lie there on the floor, her that's been taken such care of. Doctor! is it a faint? is it a faint? is it—'

Another moment of awful suspense, the silence tingling, creeping; the voices of the little crowd sounding like echoes far off. Then the doctor rose from where he had been kneeling on the floor.

'Why did you let her do this?' he said, sternly, 'I warned you she must not do it.'

'Oh, doctor, her heart was set upon it—and such a beautiful morning, and her new, beautiful fur cloak as she couldn't catch cold in. Doctor, why don't you do something? Doctor!' cried the mother, seizing him by the arm.

He shook her off. He was rough in his impatience. 'Can't you see,' he said, 'that there is nothing to be done? Take off that horrible finery; the poor girl is dead.'

'The poor girl is dead.' Grace thought it was her own voice that repeated those awful words. They went to her heart with a shock, making her giddy and faint. Her voice sounded through the confused cries of the woman about that prostrate figure. 'Dead!' The doctor turned to her, as if it was she to whom explanations were due.

'I warned them,' he said, 'that her life hung on a thread. I told them she must make no exertion. I knew very well how it would be. The wonder is that she has lasted so long,' he added, after that momentary excitement sinking into professional calm. 'No, no, there's nothing to be done. Can't you see that for yourself?'

'And the cab at the door to take her for her airing!' cried the mother, in shrill tones of distraction. 'Oh, doctor, give her something! The brandy, where is the brandy, Matilda? I've seen her as far gone—'

'You have never seen her like this before. She is dead,' said the doctor, in the unceremonious tones in which he addressed such patients. 'You had better get a sofa or something to lay her on, poor thing! nothing can hurt her now; and send and let her husband know.' He followed Grace out into the passage, where she had withdrawn, unable to bear that awful sight.

'It is a strange story. I don't understand it. Sounds like a novel,' he said. 'I don't think he'll be very sorry. He'll bear it better than most—though he only married her about three weeks ago. It was the strangest thing I ever heard of. A gentleman—no doubt of that. What he could ever have to say to a girl like her, God knows. But he suddenly appeared on the scene when she was at the last gasp, and married her. I had given her up; but afterwards she made a surprising rally. Even I was taken in. I thought that she might still pull through. But you see I was mistaken,' he added cheerfully.

Grace stood and leaned against the wall. Everything swam in her eyes, and all the sounds, the voices of the women lamenting within, the cries and questions without, the sharp, clear sentences of the doctor, all mingled in a strange confusion like sounds in a dream. In the midst of all this tumult came the voice of Trix calling to her to come out into the open air, and a touch on her arm, which she felt to be that of the doctor, leading her away. She made a great effort and recovered herself. 'We want to know,' she said, faintly, grasping at Trix's hand. 'We came to see—we belong to Mr. Wentworth,' and then with a rush of gathering energy her sight came back to her, and she saw the face of the man who stood, curious yet indifferent, between her and the chamber of death.

'Ah, the husband!' he said.

'We came—to see her: is it truly, truly—? He has been ill, and we have to act for him. We have—his authority. Trix, speak for me! Is it—? Is that—?' There came a strange, convulsive movement in her throat, like sobbing, beyond her control. She could not articulate any more.

'I am his sister,' said Mrs. Ford; 'is it true?—is the woman— dead? Oh! it's dreadful to be glad, I know. If you are the doctor, tell us, for Heaven's sake! Is she dead—is it she—the woman—'

'The poor girl,' said Grace, softly; 'the poor, poor girl!'

This she said over and over again to herself as they drove away. She made no reply to the questions, the remarks, the thanksgivings of her companions. They drove straight to the Temple in direct contradiction of Mr. Ford's orders, and went up into the chambers where Oliver had suffered so much, from which he had escaped in the half delirium of his despair. Mr. Ford was there, still inquiring vaguely, endeavouring to find some clue. He met the ladies, as was natural, with suppressed rage, asking what they wanted there; but the news they brought was sufficient even in his eyes to excuse their appearance, though even that threw no light upon the other question, which now became the most important: where Oliver had gone.

CHAPTER IX

When Oliver left his rooms on that terrible night, it could scarcely be said that he was a sane man. The strange, confused tinkling and pealing of the bell had seemed to him a supernatural call. When he had come to himself a little, out of the strange, wild fit of ridicule of himself and his pitiful intention of escaping from fate, which had overcome him, he had risen mechanically and gone to the door. When he found no one, the impulse of half-mad derision seized him again. It was as if he had gone through every possibility of the anguish and misery that were real, and had come out on the other side where all is distorted and fantastic, and nothing true; where there were voices without persons, calls, and jarring summonses that meant nothing, a chaos of delusion and self-deceit, in which fever and shattered nerves and reverberations out of a diseased brain were the only elements, and every impression was fictitious, ridiculous, mad and false. He went out without knowing what he was doing, the echoes of the pistol-shot circling through his head, and moving him again and again to wild laughter: to think

83

that he should have found himself out so! that he was such a poor creature after all, capable of running away, not good enough to stand and be executed, which was his just due. Was it to be executed that he feared, or to be banished, or put in prison, tied, yes, that was it—tied to a dead body, as other men had been before him? Whatever it was, he had not been man enough to bear his punishment, but had tried to run away. And then he had been frightened, and failed.

By this time he had forgotten altogether what expedient he had intended to adopt to make his escape by, and the report, which still echoed through his head, seemed to him rather the punishment he was attempting to escape from than the means of escape. But anyhow he was running away, and was afraid to do it. He was running away and could not do it. He was somehow caught by the foot, so that all his running and walking were vain, and he was only making circles about the fatal spot in which the executioner was waiting for him—steadily, patiently waiting—until the meshes should be drawn tighter and he should be brought back. The bell continued to peal in his brain, a mocking summons, and the report of the pistol to break in at intervals, sharp, like a refrain, bringing back more or less the first effect of re-awakening, but not to reality, only to that ever-renewed derision of his own efforts to get away. The fool that he was! How could he escape with the bands ever tightening, tightening about his feet, as he kept on in his vain round, back and back in circles that lessened, every round leading nearer and nearer to the spot where Fate awaited him, grimly looking on at his vain struggles, laughing in that fierce ridicule which he re-echoed though he carried on those sickening efforts still?

He must have carried out in reality the miserable confusion in his brain, for it seemed afterwards that he had done nothing but go round and round a circle of streets and lanes, surrounding the point where his chambers were, and where he was seen by various people, appearing and reappearing, always at a very rapid pace, through the lingering darkness of the night. After a while, in all probability, recollection failed him, for his horrible sensations seemed to fade into a dull, fatigued consciousness of circling and winding, of always the band on his ankles tightening, drawing him nearer; but no longer any clear idea of what was the impending doom, from which only this perpetual movement, this effort to keep on, saved him for a time. Finally, when daylight had come, surprising and alarming him back into some effort of intelligence, he found himself at the door of his club, where the servants were but beginning to open the shutters, to sweep and clean out, in preparation for the day. He crept in there somehow as a dog might creep into a barn, or take refuge in an empty kennel, and threw himself shivering into an easy-chair, and had a cup of coffee brought him by a compassionate waiter, who saw that he had been up all night. The same kind hands covered him up when he began in his exhaustion to doze. And there he lay and slept through all the early morning hours, while still there was nobody to comment upon his appearance or to disturb him. The servants of the club chattered indeed among themselves; they shook their heads, and said he had been up to something or other as he hadn't ought to. They suggested to each other that he had been in bad company, that he had been drugged, which was the most likely thing to account for his dazed appearance. But he lay and slept through it all, unconscious in the profound sleep of entire exhaustion. Most

85

likely it was that exhaustion and the constant physical movement and keen air of the night which saved his brain after all.

He woke at about eleven o'clock, having slept four or five hours, shivering with a nervous chill, and in all the bodily misery of a man who has slept in his clothes on a chair, cramped and wretched; but yet in full possession of his senses, and knowing everything that had happened. It all came back to him slowly, the standing trouble first, the horror of those circumstances in which he was involved, the awful question what he was to do: how live and endure his existence since he could not abandon it? He asked himself the question almost before he remembered that he had intended to abandon it. And then the scene of last evening slowly rolled back upon him like a scene in a tragedy, the crack of the pistol, the violent jarring and jingling of the bell. He could not have dreamt or imagined the bell: it must have meant some messenger or other, someone bringing him news. What news could any messenger be bringing? Nothing but one piece of news. Nothing else was worth sending now, worth the trouble of sending—his release, perhaps. Oh, Heaven! if that might be!

Oliver got up quickly in the sudden gleam of possibility thus presented to him. It aroused him from the torpor of sleep and wretchedness and exhaustion. But afterwards he dropped heavily into his chair again, shaking his head, saying to himself that it was impossible, that release did not come to a man so placed as he was, that he had no right to release. And then it occurred to him that the messenger might return and find the door open and go in, and that his letter lay on the table, the letter addressed to his brother-in-law with its confession. By this time, then, it would be in their hands and all would be known. When that thought entered his mind, he rose from his chair, not impetuously, but in the calm of despair: ah, that was best! that everything should be known. It was all over then. Whatever might happen, Grace was lost to him for ever. Whatever might happen, his own life and its hopes were over, without any possibility of redemption. 'So be it,' he said to himself, bowing his head almost solemnly: 'so be it.' What else was possible? He would at least have discharged the dreadful duty of cutting himself off, and leaving her free.

This was his real awakening—which was, though the May morning was so bright, an awakening into the blackness and darkness, into the quiet of despair—no possibility now, no hope, all over and ended for ever and ever. He took his hat and walked out without a word, without a thought of his appearance, in the fresh daylight, in the open street, unshaven, unkempt, miserable, with a misery which no one could mistake. How he appeared was no longer anything to him. He saw nobody, took notice of nothing. He might have been walking through a desert as he made his way through some of the busiest streets of London, full of traffic and commotion, and never saw one of the people who stared at the man who seemed a gentleman, and yet had such an air of haggard misery, a wanderer who had been out all night; nothing of this did Oliver see. He went doggedly to give himself up to justice—no, that was the part of the last night's dream: but, at least, to meet at last whatever might be coming to him, to ascertain that his letter had been sent away and that all was over. Everything was over, in any case; but it would all be more evident, more certain, if the letter had been sent away.

He went up his own staircase and came to his own door with nothing but this in his mind. The recollection of the bell, of the possible messenger who could not get admission, of the news of his release which might have come, all faded out of his mind. If that letter had been sent, it did not matter whether he was released or not: now or hereafter, what could it matter? so long as that letter had been sent. Then indeed his tale would be told, his shrift over, his fate sealed. He heard voices vaguely as he approached the room, but took no notice. What did it matter who was there so long as the letter had been sent? He stalked in like a ghost, his eyes fixed upon the table which seemed to him as he had left it—all but one thing.—Yes, redemption had become impossible and hope was over. The letter had gone.

'Oliver!' said a voice, whether in a dream, whether in fact, whether out of the skies, whether only sounding in the depths of his miserable heart, how could he tell? He turned round towards it slowly, pale, trembling, a man for whom hope was no more. And there she stood before him, she who had been to him as an angel, whom he had seemed to abandon, insult and betray. It seemed so; and never, perhaps, never would it be known how different—how different! He could not bear the sight of the brightness of her face. There was light in it that seemed to kill him; he put up his hands to cover his eyes, and shrank back, back, until, his limbs tottering under him, his heart failing him, he had sunk unawares upon his knees. Oh, the brightness of the presence of outraged love, more terrible than wrath! Is it not from that, that at the last the sinner, self-convicted, will flee?

'Do not speak to me,' he said, his voice sounding like some

stranger's voice in his own ears. 'I know all you would say. And there is no excuse, no excuse.'

'Oliver! you have no excuse for not trusting me. I was worthy of your trust. Should I not have chosen for you to do first what was right?'

It seemed to him that once more his brain was giving way; he felt a horrible impulse to laugh out again at the mockery of this speech. Right! there was nothing right! What had it to do with him, a man all wrong, wrong, out of life, out of hope—that there should still be some one left in the world to whom that word meant something? He uncovered his face, however, and looked up at her from out the humiliation of despair. And then he began to see that there were other people in the room, his sister, his brother-in-law, looking on at the spectacle of his downfall. He rose up slowly to his feet, supporting himself against the wall.

'I am in great distress,' he said; 'I am not able to speak. Ford, will you take them away?'

Ford, who was only a man, nobody in particular, gave him a certain sense of protection in the poignancy of the presence of the others, before whom he could not stand or speak.

'Oliver, old fellow, you needn't look so miserable; they wouldn't go, they know everything, they've got—news for you. I say they've got news for you.'

'Oh, Tom, God bless you! you have a feeling heart after all. Oliver, it is all over—'

'Oliver,' Grace put out her warm hands and took his, which

89

were trembling with an almost palsy of cold; 'I should have understood, for you told me long ago—you told me there were things I would not understand. But now I do understand. And all that you have done I approve. I do not forgive you—I approve.'

He drew back ever further, shrinking against the wall. 'I was mad last night,' he said, 'and it was horrible: and now I must be going mad again—and this is horrible too, but it is sweet—'

'Oh, it is horrible,' cried Grace, with tears; 'for it comes out of misery and mourning. Oliver, that poor girl—that poor girl, she is dead.'

He fell down once more at her feet, with a great and terrible cry, and fainted like a woman—out of misery, and remorse, and relief, and anguish, and joy, and by reason too, since the body and the soul are so linked together—of his sleepless nights and miserable days.

He told her all afterwards, in those subdued and troubled days when happiness was still struggling to come back. But Grace would never see it as he did. To her it was an atonement, an almost martyrdom. She could not understand those deeper depths of evil in which sin is taken lightly, and called pleasure, and is but for a day. She could understand passion and the deadly harm it wrought, and how life itself might be laid down in the desire to atone. He held his peace at last, bewildered by the dulness of that innocence which could not so much as imagine what he knew. And happiness did struggle back through depths of humiliation and shame to him, with which she was never acquainted. She did not suffer, not having sinned; and he was still young. And after awhile the hideous dream through which he passed faded away, and even Oliver remembered it no more.

THE END

www.ingramcontent.com/pod-product-compliance
Lightning Source LLC
Chambersburg PA
CBHW011441170626
46807CB00008B/3256